REAL MONEY
BLOODLINE SERIES
BOOK 9
By
Lynda Rees

REAL MONEY

BLOODLINE SERIES BOOK 9

By
Lynda Rees
email: lyndareesauthor@gmail.com

Website: http://www.lyndareesauthor.com

Original Edition

Copyright © 2019 by

Publisher: Sweetwater Publishing Company

6694 Ky. Hwy. 17 North, DeMossville, KY 41033

http://www.sweetwaterpublishingcompany.wordpress.com

Edited by Melinda Williams

Email: lyndareesauthor@gmail.com
Website: http://www.lyndareesauthor.com
Facebook: @lynda.rees.author

This book is dedicated to my first broker and dear friend,
Shirley Carey.
Your brilliant mind pushed my limits and challenged me.
You inspired me to strive for excellence.
I learned these and many more things from you.
I loved selling real estate,
Made friends and had fun along the way.
You taught me to set goals and
Push past them to make my dreams come true.
Love is to be cherished, never taken for granted,
And must be enjoyed every single day.
Thank you for these lessons.
I love miss you, Shirley.

CHAPTER 1

Chloe Roberts wobbled and held her head with both hands trying to keep it from falling off her neck as she stood. A deep breath and she stumbled into the bathroom where she brushed fungus growing on her teeth away. She swallowed a couple migraine-grade pain relievers. Blinking at brilliant rays of spring sunshine invading their living space, she stumbled into the kitchen.

God bless Casey.

Her best friend, Dr. Casey Martin, had left her half a pot of strong java. She poured an awaiting cup full to the brim and leaned her butt against the counter top. Sipping the healing brew, she praised the Lord, hoping her hangover wouldn't kill her.

The door flew open. Hurricane Casey bopped into the living room carrying mail. A sympathetic observation showed she was aware of Chloe's state.

"Morning, Sunshine. Did you polish off a whole bottle of wine by yourself last night? You were out like a light when I checked on you before taking my morning run. I'd hoped you'd want to join." She sorted through paperwork then laid a stack on the credenza by the door.

"Lordy, girl, I could no more run than fly. I drank two bottles."

"I'm worried. You're not a skilled drinker. You should give it up and have got to stop feeling at fault because of your fight with Hal. The cops swear it had no bearing on his disappearance." Her five-foot-ten, slender frame sauntered into the kitchen area of the great room in their shared apartment. Casey poured her own coffee.

"My inability to handle large amounts of alcohol can be counted on—if nothing else. I wasn't punishing myself by overindulging." Chloe frowned, then tip-toed and placed a peck on Casey's cheek.

Casey chuckled. "You always were a cheap drunk. Something else going on I should know about?"

"I'm slowly getting over the guilt thing. My therapist taught me a few tactics to help with the brooding. I accept I had nothing to do with Hal's situation. He wouldn't have deserted everything he owned and would've contacted his parents by now—if he could. We're all devastated. None of us had been able to find closure, and it's been over a year." She sipped her steaming cup and eyed her friend over it. "I miss Hal. I did love him. He disappeared before I had time to learn to hate him for cheating."

"I know, sweetie, and it was wise of you to seek help." Casey's head rocked sideways. "But—"

"It still hurts. That last morning during our argument he swore he loved me, too. We might never have made it work—or maybe we would've. There's no way to know." She shrugged.

Her insides crawled the way they did when she was working toward a panic attack. She stood tall, closed her eyes and took a slow, deep, cleansing breath. Her nerves calmed considerably.

"I love you, Casey. Thanks for putting up with me and my volatile moods. I appreciate you giving me a home, even if it's temporary. If it weren't for you, I'd be bunking with Mom."

"We couldn't have you living with Ava, now. Could we?" Casey wiggled a brow.

"Yeah, much as I love Mom, we'd be fussing all the time. I'm grateful to have both of you in my life. I'm getting better by the day, but yesterday I was a bundle of nerves waiting for the real estate exam results. I drowned my fear in nectar of the gods."

"You can count on me, Chloe. But seriously . . . two bottles?"

"Yeah. Popping the second cork was ridiculous. I knew when I did it. I went head first over the brink feeling sorry for myself and stressed." She brushed a palm over her face, forehead and back over her messy top-knot.

"Lucky for you the waiting is over." Casey flipped an envelope from her sweatshirt pocket and pushed it into Chloe's hands.

Chloe backed away from it with hands in the air in surrender stance. "Oh, hell no, not with a head the size of a blimp, I can't open it. You do it. Read the bad news. I'm an experienced real estate agent, but the state exam is tricky. I studied hard, but it was a tough test." Chloe ran to the couch, jumped into a corner and hugged her feet to her body sipping the hot drink. Her skin prickled, breaking into goose bumps. She was acting like a frightened child, but she didn't care. She simply could not face the writing on that note.

"You dope. You handled major, multi-billion dollar deals for three years as an agent in New York City. You can surely pass the Kentucky Exam." Casey shook her head. She sat her drink down and slit the envelope open. "Dear Ms. Chloe Roberts, we're happily to inform you; you passed the Kentucky Real Estate Test. Your grade is below along with your license number. Blah . . . blah . . . blah . . ." Casey's brows rose, and tears filled her green eyes. "You did it, girl. You're a licensed real estate agent."

Chloe grabbed the envelope perusing it quickly. Then taking Casey's elbows they hopped delightedly in a circle squealing like little girls.

"This calls for celebration—one without alcohol. Don't forget. We're bowling with Jaiden and Leo tonight. I'm anxious for you to meet them." Casey laughed.

Chloe hugged her. "Thanks, Casey. You're a real pal. I'm excited to meet your friends. Promise this isn't another attempt to set me up. I'm not ready. Besides, didn't you date Leo?" She eyed her friend tilting her face.

"Leo and I went on one date. It felt like dating my brother. Neither of us was into the other. We'd known each other through family since we were kids, though he's four years older. He's a free agent. We're better as friends."

"How do you know the gal? What's her name again?"

"Jaiden's awesome. She's gutsy, raw, and fun. She's the bravest female I know, and she's absolutely stunning. She's got this exotic aspect about her from her part-Irish, part-Choctaw heritage; a mane of thick black hair; and a wacky sense of humor. She moved here from El Paso. Jaiden was a Texas Ranger. Her bro, Cal works at Mane Lane Farm training racer horses for Levi Madison. He settled here when he retired from the Navy and brought their mom along. Jaiden followed them."

"Jaiden sounds interesting. What's Leo like?"

"He's tall with broad shoulders and slim like a runner. He works out with weights, so he's strong but can't bulk up to save his soul. He's sweet and considerate and kind. It's impossible to dislike him."

"So what you're saying is he's built okay, would make a great older brother, but he's homely as hell." Chloe snickered.

"Hell no, Leo's a cutie pie." Casey winked. "I wouldn't fix you up with a dog."

"Just as I figured." She groaned.

"Not really. Leo doesn't date much. His wife died a couple years back. He took it hard. He's lonely, but has responsibilities. I'm not sure he's ready to move on. I figured you'd like him, and the two of you might become friends. Honest, I'm innocent."

"Yeah, right." Chloe's cell rang. "Hello, oh, hi, Mom. You have perfect timing, as usual. My letter from the state board arrived. I aced the test. I'm officially a Kentucky real estate agent."

"Wonderful, Chloe. Congratulations. Come in the office tomorrow, and take phone duty. I'll give your computer access and have everything ready." Ava Roberts' voice hinted at thrilled pride fringed with relief.

"Are you psychic, or did you have another reason for calling?"

"Tomorrow's Thursday. Mom's family dinners are Thursdays. I can pick you up on my way at six."

"Geez, I figured she'd stopped that tradition by now."

"Why, sweetheart? Mom enjoys cooking. It's no fun doing it for one. She needs company and family. Maybe someday we'll be more than three, but three makes a family. She's getting up there in years. We need to spend what time we can with her. Who knows what the future brings?"

Chloe rolled her eyes at the hint that she hadn't produced a grandchild yet for Ava. "Gran's okay, isn't she?" Concern shot through Chloe. She adored Grandma Angelica Rizzo.

"She's starting to lose hearing, but is extremely touchy about it. Don't say anything, or you'll piss her off. It's messing with her thinking capabilities and memory too.

She is easily confused. Something is wrong. She's forgetful and says the strangest things. You'll see what I mean. I want your opinion. I'd like to convince her to get a thorough checkup, but need to do it tactfully, without argument. I don't want to upset her. Will you help?"

The thought of anything harming her precious grandmother angered every nerve ending in Chloe's body. Gran Angelica and Mom had been her rocks, especially since Dad tossed her and Mom aside like dirty dishrags.

"I hadn't thought about Gran aging when I went away to school then moved to New York. I guess kids expect parents and grandparents to be eternal, and not grow older while we're not looking. I'm anxious to see her. Thanks, Mom. See you tomorrow."

CHAPTER 2

The bowling alley was retro pink and white fiberglass and neon. Dim lighting and fifties-sixties music muffled continual strikes of hard balls rumbling along lanes then crashing into pins. Automatic machines swept pins away to be reset. The occasional 'whoop' or clap sounded in the busy melee of festivities. Sweaty shoe odor mingled with nachos, popcorn, stale beer and a distinctive scent such establishments offered.

"It has been years since I bowled." Chloe shivered, as she and Casey donned awkward, rented shoes. At least she'd worn thick socks.

"I love bowling, but don't get much time for it. Lanes are largely taken by competition teams. We're lucky to get an available one tonight." Casey smiled as she tied her laces "Here they come now."

Casey hugged the petite, dark-skinned female. Her mane of black curls had been tamed into a thick ponytail flipping behind her gorgeous head. Her hourglass figure poured into a five-foot-two frame. The gal turned toward her with a friendly smile. A horse-head tattoo became visible on the side of her neck.

"Chloe, meet my friend, Jaiden Coldwater. Jaiden and Leo are two of Sheriff Wyatt Gordon's deputies. She's somewhat of a local hero. Jaiden made a big impression right away when she moved to Sweetwater, helping Wyatt close a huge case."

Jaiden stepped forward and shook Chloe's hand heartily. She might be petite, but there was nothing shy or backward about Jaiden. "I'm happy to finally meet you, Chloe. This one talks about you all the time." She waved toward Casey.

"Same here, Jaiden, I'm happy to meet a hometown hero. Casey's said great things about you." Chloe stood barely taller than the policewoman.

Casey put her glittering purple ball on the track. "Chloe and I are like sisters and have been pals since we wore diapers."

"I don't know about the hero thing. I came here a wounded bird after a drug bust in Texas because Mom was eager to nurse me back to health. I took the job with Wyatt at perfect timing. He needed an unknown face to infiltrate a drug gang. After that, this incredible community took me in and healed me. I finally found where I belong."

"With the right clothing and makeup, and the help of that tattoo on your neck, you could look like a gang banger." Chloe smiled and winked in Jaiden's direction. "Is that why you got the tat—to look tough?"

Jaiden pulled her collar down so Chloe could better see her body art. "No, but you're right. It helped make me look sinister. Actually, my horse died. I'd had him since I was a toddler learning to ride. Old Sampson was special, and I got the artwork done in his honor." Jaiden sat beside Chloe and flipped her curls back.

"Jaiden's fiancé, Clay Barnes, is a surgeon at Sweetwater General. We work together sometimes. He's on duty tonight." Casey stretched her arms.

"Doc's filling in for someone, so here I am." Jaiden slipped spike-heeled boots off and stepped into her bowling shoes.

"I look forward to meeting Clay." Chloe felt instant kinship with the friendly deputy. Her shoulders began to relax. This was what she needed—a low key night out with friends, and an opportunity to form new ties. Soon this place would feel like home again. Maybe then Chloe would stop feeling like a lost soul.

While Jaiden and Chloe talked, the jean and tee shirt clad, crew-cut fellow lifted Casey off the floor. She was a couple inches taller than Chloe but no match to the tall, good looking man. Muscles bulged in his slim arms as he spun her around. Her feet flew out joyously, and she cackled joyously.

"How's my favorite doctor?" A genuine grin attested to their close friendship.

Sitting his target gently aground, Leo released Casey. He turned, and his winning smile shown on Chloe. Those adorable emerald color eyes locked with hers as though looking straight into her soul. It frightened and excited her at the same time.

"Casey can't stop talking about her friend, Chloe. It's about time we met you." A hand extended her way. Bending his long frame, he moved closer, eye-to-eye with her, where she'd sat beside Jaiden.

She stood barely taller than shoulder-height to the hunky, blonde *Opey Taylor*. She'd lay odds a younger Leo had sported a display of freckles across his cute, straight nose. Leo resembled a grown Ron Howard and seemed as sweet and sincere. Casey had mentioned he'd suffered rough times. He had obviously weathered life's burdens with a survivor's good attitude.

17

Instantly liking the precocious male who bubbled over with joy, Chloe shook his hand eagerly. "Nice meeting you, Leo. I've heard awesome things about you and Jaiden from Casey." His firm, warm hand felt nice. She couldn't recall the last time a man had touched her, even her hand—maybe the FBI agent who had assisted her when she collapsed hearing about Hal.

Leo's cool, ocean breeze scent fit his personality. His raspy voice and exuberant spirit endeared him to her. She needed positive people overflowing with lust for life in her world. Leo was like a fresh spring breeze washing away stale winter airs as it filtered through a window. His intense stare ensured he had ample interest in Chloe as well. She had a hunch Leo sported a big heart beneath appealing, slender muscle and sinew.

Nodding, he folded his long frame into a seat and slung a duffel bag beside him. Whipping it open he pulled out personal footwear. "We are indeed awesome. I'd expect no less from Casey. Doc can't tell a lie."

"I wouldn't dare fib about the town's most fabulous law-enforcement team. You could act a little more humble." Casey stuck her tongue out at Leo before doing a practice throw knocking down nine pins.

Jaiden shook her head dubiously rolling her eyes as she shoved expensive cowboy boots into her bag. She shrugged pointing at Leo. "I don't know about this dude. I, myself am not too shabby." She grinned conspiratorially and winked at him.

He shoved her shoulder playfully.

She gently slapped Leo's hand turning to Casey and Chloe. "Thanks for inviting us tonight, gals. With Doc tied up, I was on my own. It's been a boring day. The single call I answered was a loose horse on a quiet country lane. I need fun, good company, greasy junk food, exercise and a few *brewskis*." She placed her ball into the turnstile in their lane and signaled for a waitress to stop by their lane.

"I know what you mean. I answered two calls. A cat got stuck in a pine tree. I climbed the damned tree. I'll be dog-gone, if the dang kitten didn't high-tail it out beating me to the ground." Leo chuckled then placed his ball on the equipment. His adorable southern drawl was soft as a summer night breeze. Chloe could listen all evening, not caring what he said.

Chloe stepped onto the platform picked the ball she'd selected up and stumbled backward. Leo spun and snatched her before she did a header toward the lower level floor. Arms secured her against him with her ball penned between. A slow grin eased across his face reminding her of a devilish boy about to do something silly.

Their eyes locked. His aura seeped through her from each spot they connected. Every cell in her body sparked to attention. She warmed through and through like one does standing too close to burning embers of a backyard campfire. A more wanton woman would nuzzle cozily beneath his chin. Her heart told her to, but Chloe wasn't as bold.

Her face fired. *How embarrassing to blush like a school girl?* Why couldn't she flirt like a normal woman? She deeply inhaled and rocked her shoulders back.

He snickered eying her up and down. His expression proved he was enjoying holding his captive. Chloe didn't mind either.

"You two bowling or getting a room?" Jaiden chuckled from the scoring table.

"Ah, sorry. Thanks for catching me, Leo. I can be an oaf at times." Embarrassment waned as she spoke and distanced herself from the man she was drawn to. She wouldn't mind those muscles gripping her tightly again sometime soon.

"Hard to believe. You look well put together to me." He winked releasing his grip. "Let's check your ball." She rolled it around so he could see the weight. "I think it's too heavy." He snatched it and strutted to a stand behind their booth. She followed, two-stepping to keep up. Balls of every size were displayed. Leo examined a purple orb for balance before extending it to her. "Try this one."

Sliding fingers into holes she test-swung it. Her small hand and slim fingers fit perfectly into the ball. "Wow, it makes a huge difference. This one's perfect. Thanks, Leo. Its years since I played. I won't be much competition. I'm sure I'll be terrible."

"You'll do fine." The lanky gent wearing a satisfied grin snatched her hand in his huge mitt and led her to their booth. Heat sifted into her skin from his touch. She longed to reach down and unfold it, if only to examine the palm to see if it glowed hot. When he released her, her paw felt deserted and lonely, having enjoyed being cradled securely.

Chloe stood on the platform, aimed as gracefully as possible and strutted toward the line swinging as she released her grasp. The colorful sphere sped along the lane. It slammed into the line of pins with a clatter. Eight fell, leaving two on the left. Her ball returned into position. She aimed again, strolled to the line and bending threw it. It wobbled, swerved and headed for the remaining pens knocking them over.

Shocked, she spun and jumped into the air clapping her hands. Her friends joined the applause and did a round of high-fives as Chloe took her seat. "I'm not so bad after all."

"I figure you for a ringer." Leo nodded watching Jaiden take a practice run at the pens. "You're on my team. We'll play Jaiden and Casey. Okay?" Everyone agreed. Chloe's heart did a double tap at the handsome deputy selecting her.

The whole evening Leo was charming, considerate and easy-going. His quirky sense of humor struck Chloe's funny bone, keeping her in stitches. By evening's end her ribs ached from laughter—maybe some from using muscles she hadn't exercised in years. Chloe and Leo barely beat Jaiden and Casey three out of four games. Afterward, the foursome drank a couple of beers s in the bar before calling it a night.

Chloe's heart ached at the evening coming to a close, but they had to work the next day. Hugging Jaiden as they stepped into brisk spring air, Chloe smiled. "This was a blast. I can't wait to meet your fella."

Jaiden's eyes glistened in the neon lights. "You'll love Doc. He's a Brainiac and bit of a nerd, all heart and cute as a newborn colt. We'll get together soon."

"Sounds good." She waved as Jaiden strolled toward her truck.

Leo released Casey from a bear hug then opened his arms to Chloe. She timidly stepped into them. They enveloped her like a warm, cozy blanket, comfortable and right. Her head rested against his chest, and his heart beat into her ear joining her pulse's throb. It had been over a year since she'd felt so alive.

He smelled like the ocean with a tint of something uniquely Leo. Inhaling, his essence filled her with longing to spend more time with him. She suspected Leo was like fine wine with many layers making up a delightful bouquet. She longed for the opportunity to peel back layers and learn what made the intriguing man tick.

Her head tilted backward as she glanced into glistening green eyes, suspecting he experienced similar emotions. His smile wrinkled tiny lines beside his eyes adding character to an already good-natured appearance. He winked as though conspiring on some unspoken topic before freeing Chloe. Cold and lonely, more so than before, she shrugged and stepped away trying to read his thoughts.

"Good night, Chloe. Would it be okay if I call you?"

Hope sparked, and a quick gasp balanced her world. "That would be lovely, Leo. I look forward to it." Jaiden and Leo had exchanged numbers with Chloe earlier.

Leo escorted them to Casey's car. He waved as he trotted a few spaces and climbed into his vehicle. Chloe laughed. The bright yellow Jeep perfectly fit the man.

"Nice going. Leo's into you. You don't appear to mind." Casey chortled climbing in her car and starting the engine.

"What's to mind? The dude's adorable. Not only is he eye-candy. He's funny and playful." She glared at her friend tilting her head.

"You two are a good fit. I knew you'd get on well." Casey snickered.

"Great, so you successfully set me up with someone I'm interested in. Thank you, Casey." She twisted her mouth then grinned. "You sure; you won't mind if he asks me out, and I go?" She wagged her brows.

"Not at all; you would be great for each other." They had a jovial laugh.

♥♥♥♥

"Have fun?" Leo's mother asked grabbing her purse and keys heading for the door.

"Sure did. It was the best evening I've had in a long time. Thanks for watching, Cy. How was your evening together?" He kissed her cheek.

"That boy's a charmer, like his daddy. I adore him and love being with him. After dinner I swung him out back. He took a long bath then went out like I'd doped him with Valium. He should be good for the night."

"Thanks, Mom. You know I appreciate it. I feel bad asking you to babysit when I'm not working. You do so much for us already. I don't know what Cy and I would do without you."

"No problem, Leo. You need to be with adults outside of work, and you need people to talk with besides a toddler. You're a wonderful daddy. Cy is thriving and lucky to have you. Don't fret so much. I'm always happy to help when I can." She pecked his cheek then shut the door behind her.

Leo locked it and leaned against the counter top. A sliver of a silver moon sparkled high in the starry sky. He had enjoyed himself more than he had in years, more than he'd anticipated. Casey hadn't been wrong. Chloe Roberts was a pleasant surprise.

Life without Claire had been a challenge. He missed her more than he'd thought possible. Watching her final days of agony had been painful, but she was at peace now. Thank goodness they had Cy before Claire became ill. Working full time and caring for their baby had been all consuming.

He'd barely lived outside of work and home during those few years. He rarely went out with friends. If it wasn't for Jaiden's and Casey's constant harassment, he'd never make time for leisure activities.

Meeting Chloe sparked something in him he'd considered long dead. He enjoyed the perky agent's quirky sense of humor and bouncy personality. She was adorable in a petite, rounded fashion. His hands itched for his palms to slide across her soft curves melding into one another. That mop of golden brown curls bounced with her every move, enticing his fingers to latch into them and pull her voluptuous lips upward so he could bend to kiss them.

Are they as delicate as they look? Would she taste as sweet as she seems?

He shook his head in wonder—back to reality. He'd need to make arrangements to accommodate more free time, if he wanted to pursue the spunky newcomer. And he did. *Yes.* He surely did.

♥♥♥♥

When Chloe woke the following morning Casey was waiting. A balloon, notepad and pen lay on the counter. "Sit. It's time you get closure with Hal. Write him a note saying everything you want him to know and say goodbye. Stick it in the balloon and blow it up. We're going in the courtyard so you can say your final whatever to your lost love. Then you'll be free from ties binding you to him. It's a closure ritual I learned from my friend Sage."

Chloe hugged her thoughtful friend. "It feels weird knowing you discussed my issues with someone I haven't met, but I love the idea. Let's do it." She pecked Casey's cheek then hopped onto the barstool and began to write.

Casey poured them coffee then sat quietly beside her. "She's a great gal. I can't wait for you to meet her. Her full name is Lemon Sage Gordon, Wyatt's wife and the product of sixty's flower children. Sage knows all sorts of cool, metaphysical things."

Chloe's mouth flew open. "It's odd thinking of our sexy, silver-haired sheriff married—and to a hippie. Who would've guessed?"

Nodding with laughter Casey took a sip. "Yep, Sage was born in a commune in upper New York State. She's an awesome woman. They're a great match."

"I'm sure she is. Wyatt fell for her." Chloe read the note one last time.

'Dear Hal. I will love you forever. I'm eternally grateful for our time together. You're gone, and I'm still here. I wish you were around, but you aren't. I'm building a new life without you. I hope you're at peace wherever you are. All my love, Chloe.'

She tied the balloon with her message inside, followed Casey out back then released it. It floated sideways for a while before a gust swooshed it high into the air.

Casey slid her arm around Chloe, and she did the same. They sipped their hot drinks, clinging together until the bright red plastic orb drifted out of sight.

"Thank you, Casey. I am grateful for your thoughtfulness, and I appreciate you more than you'll ever know. You're a thoughtful friend. You were right. I can't believe how much better I feel already." Hal had disappeared before she'd had opportunity to speak her heart completely. She would never again hesitate to tell people she cherished how she felt ab

CHAPTER 3

Angelica Roberts had set the table for dinner with candles and her finest china, crystal, silverware and linens. Chloe helped Ava serve the food.

"Is this festivity for my benefit, to welcome me home to Sweetwater?" Chloe stretched her five-foot-one-inch frame on tiptoes to peck Angelica's cheek. Gran stood five-ten, slim and still shapely at the advanced age of eighty.

"I'm thrilled you finally moved home where you belong. We've missed you."

Chloe loved making her grandmother smile. Her face was even more beautiful with a glisten in her eye.

"The lasagna smells delightful." Ava sat and poured her mother and daughter glasses of red wine. Angelica's slender, manicured fingers served portions with slices of buttery garlic bread.

"I'll gain weight eating like this." Chloe winced soaking in delectable fragrance. "Gran, how do you stay in perfect shape?" She'd long admired her grandmother's sleek physique.

"It's your favorite, Chloe. Enjoy, and thank you, darling. I don't' eat this way every day, and I participate in three water-aerobic classes each week. Muscle memory easily maintains my dancer's body. Years on stage help a performer stay fit forever." Angelica looked pleased with herself and proud of Chloe's admiration.

"I wish I'd seen you perform. You must've been something." Wistfully, she'd missed spending time with family. It was good being home. "You're beautiful now. I can imagine how spectacular you looked on stage as a young woman."

Angelica smiled sweetly. Her silver bob moved with her head. No hair dared fall out of place on the perfectly coiffed, regal lady. "Young people are beautiful. Your grandpa always says I was a sight to behold on stage. We early Radio City Rockettes were considered the most talented, beautiful and glamorous women in New York, if not the country. Only the best of the best made it into the troop. Your grandpa preened sporting me around on his arm."

"I'll bet he was proud. Was he good looking?" Gran rarely spoke about him, probably due to her missing him terribly.

Angelica placed a silky hand atop Chloe's. "Oh, he is, Chloe. He's the most elegant, handsome man I ever met. His tall, muscular frame has a rippling belly and broad shoulders with hair dark as mine. We have always looked the perfect couple."

"Did you lead an exciting life in New York?" The story was intriguing. She'd never thought to query Gran about her early years.

Sipping wine Angelica smiled as though reminiscing. "Indeed, we did. We ran in a fast, high-society crowd with powerful, influential personalities including celebrities. People liked Grandpa and wanted to be seen with him. They tried to remain on his good side. We partied constantly with famous folks and went to the best clubs like the Tropicana. We danced to Latin music at the Palladium

Dance Hall. Grandpa was quite the dancer. Grandpa was friends with the owner of The Cotton Club where we danced to Jazz. People called him *The Killer*. It was an exciting, daring time when everyone dressed elegantly to go out."

"I suppose he'd have to be in order to attract a professional like you, Mom." Ava smiled proudly at her mother.

Angelica didn't blush, obviously used to such praise. She went about her meal.

Chloe's interest had sparked fond reminiscing. *Maybe it's a way to test Gran's memory issues.*

"So you knew a lot of celebrities, Gran. Would I recognize any of them?"

"Oh, sure. Whenever they came to town famous folks liked to run around with Grandpa and me. I especially enjoyed those young actors they called the *Rat* something or other. Frankie, Dean, Tony and the little black fella . . . ummm . . . Sammy—yeah that's it. That Dean character was a dreamboat, but he didn't play around on his wife like some did. He had a reputation as a boozer, but he rarely drank like the others. He expertly pretended to be drunk when the need called for it. He was a convincing actor and a sweet thing. They were a fun bunch." Gran wagged her brows and winked.

Chloe laid her fork down in awe. "Gran, do you mean the *Rat Pack*—Frank Sinatra, Dean Martin, Tony Bishop and Sammy Davis, Jr.?" She could hardly believe what she heard.

"Yes, that's them. They sure knew how to party." She could've been discussing a grocery list, as casual as she acted about knowing the infamous stars.

"Wow, Mom, I didn't realize you knew such famed celebrities." Ava's eyes grew wide, and she wore an incredulous expression.

"Now, Ava, your mother had a life before your birth. I was a renowned dancer. Of course, I ran with a fast crowd."

Ava's brows rose and fell as Angelica gave her attention to Chloe. "Enough about me. Chloe, I want to hear about you and your young man. Is he moving to Sweetwater?"

Chloe swallowed hard. The bite she'd taken dropped into her gut like a brick. A sip of wine, then she dotted her eyes with a napkin.

Thank goodness for waterproof mascara.

"Mother, I told you Chloe's young man disappeared a year back. No one's seen Hal Spence since he left one day for the gym. Even his parents remain at a loss for what happened. Chloe sold her condo and moved home." Ava patted her mother's fragile looking hand.

Angelica blinked away confusion flashing across her face. "I'm sorry, Chloe. I knew. It slipped my mind. I didn't mean to make you cry. Please forgive an old woman." Her tone filled with sympathy.

"It is okay, Gran. Forget it. Life goes on. I've relocated and obtained my real estate license. I'm starting to work for Mom."

"Wonderful news, we can see more of you now you're living in town. Where are you staying, with your mother?"

"No, I'm bunking in Casey Martin's spare room until I get on my feet. I'll find a small house to buy, once I make some sales."

"Perfect. Now we need to find you a good man." Angelica patted Chloe's hand.

It should be so easy.

Giving Gran a brilliant smile, Chloe stowed the depressing conversation behind them. "I'm happy being here, Gran. Please, no match-making. I can barely keep up with the fellas Casey trots in front of me. We went bowling last night with her friends Jaiden and Leo. Jaiden is a gal, but Leo is single and seemed really nice."

Ava's attention perked, and she smiled. "Jaiden Coldwater and Leo Sanders?"

Chloe nodded. "They're friends of Casey's and work together at the sheriff's department as deputies. Leo grew up in Sweetwater, but he's a few years my senior. I don't remember him from school."

"I'm familiar with them, dear. Jaiden moved here a few years back. They're good people." Ava pretended to eat, but Chloe saw she was trying to not look eager about her daughter meeting a man she approved of.

"Jaiden is engaged to Dr. Clay Barnes." Chloe savored another bite of lasagna.

"Yes, Clay returned to Sweetwater a couple years ago. Leo is unattached, far as I know. You liked him?" Ava's brow rose, and she glanced sideways at Chloe with hope in her eyes.

"Sure. They're super." She avoided Ava's ploy.

"Is Casey trying to fix you up with Leo?" Angelica cocked her head not appearing surprised.

She squirreled her mouth to the side. "Maybe. I guess. Leo seemed like a great guy. What do you think?"

"Leo's a wonderful young man. He's very responsible. Keep an open mind, darling." Ava turned attention to her mother. "You know, Mom, it's great you stay in touch with your card group for monthly lunches and exercise regularly. We women must take care of ourselves. It's a long time since I've gotten a complete physical. I should schedule one for all three of us to get checked out. We can make a day of it with our appointments, lunch in the antique district and a bit of shopping. Up for it, Mom? Chloe?" She pointedly eyed Chloe, prompting her support.

Catching on quickly Chloe didn't hesitate—grateful the subject of her single status had been diverted. "Great idea, Mom, it's been awhile since I've had an exam. Let's do it. Okay, Gran?"

Angelica shrugged. "I suppose. I can't recall having a physical either."

"Good. I'll make arrangements and let you both know when we're set." Mom acted relieved, having jumped a hurdle.

♥♥♥♥

On the ride home Chloe played with Ava's controls trying to find a station she could tolerate. "Don't you listen to anything but talk radio?"

"It's my car, Chloe. I listen to what I like."

"You played Gran smoothly tonight. You're right. Something is going on. She forgot about Hal . . . She's never acted so open talking about her past and Grandpa. I don't recall her doing that before. Maybe she did, and as a kid I didn't pay attention."

"No, you're right. She drifts more and more into distant past. She was always evasive and hated talking about Dad since he died when I was young. I don't remember him. No matter how much I asked as a kid, all I got was, '*He was handsome, smart, charming and a powerful businessman.*'"

"What type business?" Chloe had never given him much thought. He simply wasn't there, and she'd focused on those who were. Their earlier conversation made her realize she knew little about family members as individuals.

"Who knows? He was an *entrepreneur, investor, and manager*— whatever that means. I figured it was hard for her to talk about losing the love of her life."

"You noticed she spoke of him in today's terms. She said, 'he is.'"

Ava nodded her way sadly.

"Did she date? I don't recall Gran having a fellow."
Weird—regal Gran dating . . .

"No. She keeps an active social life. She always dressed well and went out a lot, I assumed with women friends. I never met or saw her with a man. I guess Dad was enough. She never wanted another love after he was gone."

"She remembers details from her far past fairly well."

"Yes, but little things like whether she had breakfast, or what she ate slip her mind. That's an early symptom of dementia. It worries me. I'm afraid she's developing Alzheimer's."

"What's the difference?" Chloe exhaled deeply, growing more and more concerned for her beloved grandmother.

"I'm not sure; but from what I gather, Alzheimer's has to do with dead spots in the brain and electrical currents not functioning properly. Dementia is progressive loss of memory in the elderly—not a specific illness. It can have many causes. Alzheimer's is a specific disease, irreversible and not curable. It's progressive and scares the hell out of me thinking she might have it."

Chloe touched her mother's shoulder. "Oh, Mom, it sounds awful. It's sad. Gran talks of legends from her past, but can't recall her hairdresser's name." She wiped a tear with the back of her sleeve. "We're in it together. I'm here for you and Gran—whatever happens." Chloe grabbed her mother's hand and held on tight.

They had stayed close. It was good she'd moved home. She had more important concerns than dwelling on her issues. Her family needed her more than she'd realized— maybe more than she needed them.

CHAPTER 4

Chloe sat in the center of a row row of partitioned spaces along a bank of windows. Her cubical barely accommodated a desk with two guest chairs and was separated by five-foot-tall glass walls.

Ava perched on the top of her desk with a smile. "Our corporate technology expert assigned configured your computer and assigned you a temporary password. The photographer shot me your corporate photos to approve for the company website and advertising. They're quite flattering and professional. He forwarded them to the marketing department and will mail you a few copies for your files." They'd spent a few hours discussing processes and promotion.

"Thanks; he showed me the proofs, and I agree. They were nice. I built my profile page and uploaded the electronic copy he sent me."

"Great; you're off to a good start." Ava laid a hand on Chloe's shoulder as she hopped off the desktop and walked to the front lobby to greet a client.

Taking phone duty for the day in lieu of her mother hadn't been productive for Chloe so far. She had answered and redirected incoming calls mostly for other agents. Not a single new customer inquiry came in. At least becoming the new office phone operator gave her time to get acclimated and meet agents filtering through the as schedules allowed.

Ring.

"Roberts Real Estate Agency, Chloe Roberts, how may I help you?"

A deep-throated, masculine growl filtered into her ear with a bit of a New York accent and some inflection she couldn't pinpoint. "Ms. Roberts, I'm happy to catch you in. You were recommended by a business associate. My name is Tray Ackerson. I'm moving to Sweetwater and need to purchase a home. There's a house on Jay Bird Lane I'd like to see. Could you show it to me?"

"I'm sure I can. Give me a second to find it in the system and schedule a tour. When would you like to view it?"

"Today's great if possible. I'm flexible." His voice was pleasant and easy.

The Multiple Listing Service showed it was listed by an agent in her office. She pulled and printed the listing records and documents in the system.

"You're talking about 25 Jay Bird?" Her heart did a happy dance.

"That's the one. It's near completion."

"Yes, and it's vacant. We should be able to get in today. It's listed at seven-hundred-fifty-thousand. How will you pay for the home?" *Please let this guy have good credit.* A sale like that would provide a decent payday, which she needed badly.

"Cash."

Words an agent loves to hear. "Great. You'll need proof of funds to submit it with an offer, should you make one."

"No problem. I'll bring it with me."

She loved working with prepared buyers. "I'll schedule the showing and meet you there at five thirty. Does that work?"

After exchanging contact information, she hung up. Her mother exited her office saying goodbye to her customer in time to catch Chloe doing a celebration jig beside her cube.

"What's going on?" She sidled over.

"I'm showing 25 Jay Bird to a cash buyer this evening." She couldn't control excitement in her voice and on her face.

Her mother glowed with joy. "That's awesome. It's not often an agent gets a showing, much less a sale the first day or even the first week. A cash buyer means a quick closing, so a fast paycheck; and you'll receive a substantial commission. Congratulations and good luck. I'll keep my fingers crossed." Ava hugged Chloe then left her to prepare for the appointment.

I might get my home sooner than I thought.

Chloe drove her SUV into the swanky, gated community and onto a freshly laid concrete driveway. Massive red brick sported shudders on front windows of the traditional style, eight bedroom, ten bathroom building.

A small, beat up truck parked in front of the garage doors. Landscaping hadn't been finished, and no sidewalks led to the house. No way to enter the nearly completed structure without trudging through thick, rutted mud.

Her three-inch heels and dress were out of place in the messy erection site. She wasn't about to track gunk through a fabulous building with freshly laid carpeting and expensive, Italian tile flooring.

A model-perfect man about six-two climbed from the pickup and strode toward her as she stepped out of her vehicle. Wearing a plaid flannel shirt beneath brown bib overalls with well-worn work boots and no hat; the guy didn't look the type to plop down three-thirds-of-a-mil on a house. He couldn't be her wealthy customer and was probably a worker ready to leave.

A camouflage ball cap rested on his dashboard. A thick head of perfectly cropped, dark hair put final touches on the hunk of masculinity headed her way. His friendly grin charmingly showed off perfect pearly whites. Tiny wrinkles formed along outsides of glistening, deep brown eyes. A thick, five-o'clock shadow framed his rugged face and broad, square jaw.

"You must be Ms. Chloe Roberts. I'm Tray Ackerson; happy to meet you." This dude wasn't at all what she'd expected.

She was a professional and hid her surprise with a glowing smile. Appearances could be deceiving. She shook his firm grip heartily—not a good idea to let him know what she was thinking.

"Good evening, Mr. Ackerson. Is this the one you wanted to see?" He didn't seem the elegant household type. There was a lot of space in the property. He and his wife must have kids or liked to entertain. The property was built for crowds.

Glancing at the structure with a brow cocked, he grinned. "Yep, it's the one. I've heard it's nice and would meet my needs. I'm not sold, but I'm anxious to check it out. It's a lot of house for a guy with no wife or kids. I'm not a party type of guy, though I occasionally entertain for business."

Pulling a paper from his pocket, he handed it to her. "Here you go. This should work for making an offer. Right? I stopped by the bank before meeting you and told the manager to only show a figure sufficient as proof of funds for the list price."

It got better and better. It didn't appear he intended to haggle. She perused the letter. The signature she recognized guaranteed Mr. Ackerson had enough cash at First National Bank of Sweetwater.

"They can close within three days of a contract, once I find the right property."

"Wonderful." She leaned into the vehicle with her backside to him to tuck the note in a file on the car seat. Turning she caught him in the act and yanked her skirt down smoothly. He didn't blush and made no excuse for eying her behind.

She trotted around back of her vehicle and whipped out a duffel bag. Stepping from her heels, she donned rubber goulashes,slipped a flashlight into her over-sized tote, and tossed in lawn bags she grabbed from a carton.

"Okay. We're ready." She set out for the building.

Mr. Ackerson snickered while studying her actions with hands on hips and a muse of awe on his face. He followed her toward the entrance. "I understand you sold real estate in New York. You didn't prepare for this situation hocking high-rise condos." He two-stepped to keep up, approaching the end of the concrete strip closest to the structure.

"No, it comes from riding on home tours with my mother since I was five. Spring rains bring mud at new construction. The last thing I want is to undo fine work the builders put into a home."

"As a buyer, I appreciate your consideration. As a contractor, I find it spot on. You impress me for someone so young in the business."

"This isn't my first rodeo, Mr. Ackerson." People sometimes commented she looked young for her age. She attributed it to Grandma Angelica's genes.

She carefully picked her way through gooey clots toward the elegant entryway then flipped out an electronic device. It signaled the lock box to open. She removed a key, inserted I; and the door swung wide. Instead of holding it for him to enter, she propped her buttocks on the ledge, removed footwear, spread a trash bag behind her, and placed her nasty boots on it. She spun around on her hind-end and stood in the foyer in as ladylike a fashion as she could manage without flashing her privates at her client. She indicated for him to do the same.

He snickered, shrugged then followed her actions. Of course, he didn't have to worry about showing his ass in its fine glory; though she wouldn't have minded seeing it. From what she discerned through heavy-duty, work pants, he had a fine specimen.

"Nice maneuver, Ms. Roberts. Well played. You're a pro ready for anything."

She led him through a massive vestibule flanked by walls of glass enclosing a study and library or office. They entered an enormous great room. The far wall of glass spanning from second floor to basement was visible showing off a partially wooded area providing privacy. One could stand at a railing and view the family room below or hallway above.

The living area spread to the right showing off a floor-to-second-floor ceiling, rock fireplace. "This room easily accommodates three full-sized couches and four contrasting, cushy chairs without looking crowded." She patted the back of the elegant sofa that probably cost as much as her vehicle.

He nodded without speaking or changing his noncommittal gaze as he meandered left toward the open dining area defined by a chandelier over a table set for ten. He made no comment as he eyed the stainless, gourmet kitchen separated by two stone-topped islands with one sporting six expensive bar stools.

"The house isn't finished, but they've done a bang up job staging it." She lingered, scanning a hand across smooth, black marble, wishing she had opportunity to cook in such a stylishly designed room.

He sauntered to railing, better taking in the view through the three-story wall of glass panels. Muddy, choppy acreage nearby opened to bluegrass-covered, rolling terrain undisturbed by equipment and bordered by peaceful background of thick hardwoods. The end of the street lot provided privacy with no homes being constructed behind or nearby on either side. Chloe couldn't have planned the showing more perfectly if she'd ordered the purple and pink sunset herself.

"This is a lovely view." She released an easy sigh.

He nodded without comment then traipsed past the cooking area without due inspection. The corridor led past a gigantic butler's pantry with walls of drawers and cabinets, an elegant guest bathroom, then through a glass-walled breezeway and up steps to an apartment over a three-car garage. With a quick inspection of the two-roomed suite and its bathroom, he trotted back downstairs.

She followed trying to match his long strides. Bare feet patting steps was the only sound echoing the walls. At the foot of the stairs he opened a door and glanced into the garage. He shut it before moving quickly through the seating area of the great room to the other side of the house. Identical-but-opposite staircases on either side of a far wall led to a second floor.

Tray moved at lightning speed. Obviously this wasn't the house for Mr. Ackerson. Most folks liked spending quality time perusing a space and figuring how their things would fit into it. This man was on a mission—likely to culminate in an unsuccessful deal.

With long legs and quick stride, he beat her to every room; and as he pushed doors open and flipped lights on, he scanned each bed and bath before reversing the process. Finally he paused long enough to thoroughly inspect a huge master suite.

41

Windows and French doors led to a private balcony. Three windows lined one side. The bedroom was well staged.

"The California king-sized bed fits well in this vast space." It was elegantly made with pricey furnishings and bedding with a fake fur throw casually draped across a corner. "The space is inviting. It makes me want to lounge and linger here." She watched his blank expression as she recited puffery.

"The bathroom is luxurious." It must've cost more than the New York condo Chloe recently sold. "There are two walk-in closets with private dressing rooms, built in vanities, shoe closets and tons of drawers, shelves and hanging space. Most women dream of such closets."

He awarded her a rare chuckle. "They do, do they?"

She shrugged, smiled, opened a door then led him along a discrete hallway with several screens and a control panel at a desk. She pulled on a volume from a bookshelf. It angled downward causing the bookcase to slide automatically aside revealing a hidden room.

"The panic room is designed with a security system managed from the outside or inside panel. If inside access is activated, outside control is disabled; and police are notified immediately of an intruder. The screen projects on the wall. A land-line plugged into the outlet is secondary to the cell phone. There is no way to deactivate this line from outside the building. You can access visuals of any property location from this space, and it projects on the wall. Impressive, don't you think?" She eyed him curiously fumbling with controls. He snickered, nodded then exited.

She followed along the nearest staircase to the lower level where he scanned storage rooms, a mirrored exercise room and an entertainment room complete with ping pong and pool tables, video games and old fashioned slot machines.

"The home theater sports a massive screen, projection equipment and seating for twenty. She waved an arm as she passed it and opened wood-slatted swinging doors so he could walk inside. "The Irish tavern has several built-in, wooden booths and a bar with stained glass decor, and is perfect for small gatherings."

He followed as she led to another open area. "The enormous family room adjoins a bathroom, which is also accessed from the rear, pool-side patio." She opened the powder room door and waltzed past a large vanity; glass-walled, over-sized shower stall and water closet, before opening a rear door."

He peeked outside and nodded, not appearing impressed with the Olympic-sized pool and Italian tiled patio.

She waltzed outside pointing to stairs and decking above. "This lower level, outdoor living space is complete with cushy seating, a fire pit and stainless kitchenette. The oval pool has exquisitely ornately tile. Once landscaping is completed, surrounding muddy area will be gone."

He nodded without a word and sped up the outside stairs. Racing to keep up, Chloe trotted behind. The deck above was similarly adorned with furnishings for lounging and meal preparation.

"The lovely view is even more impressive from here as from the living room." She sighed catching her breath, finally slowing down. She was getting nowhere with this fella.

"You're right. It's nice. I'm not thrilled with the house." His mouth screwed to the side. "I need a home fast. I was hoping this would work." Finally his blank face showed emotion.

There it is.

It wasn't what she'd hoped for, but even disappointment provided hope. She'd figured as much. "Tell me your thoughts." She plopped on a sofa sinking into its indulging cushion.

He sat across from her. "The house is large, and that's not bad. I don't need near this amount of space, but am not against it. My partner and I frequently have out-of-town guests, so we could use it occasionally. Dark wood throughout and thick trim aren't my style, and even the elaborate kitchen feels dreary, though plenty of outside light streams through. It has an old-fashioned vibe that doesn't suit me. I prefer more modern and less formal."

She longed to touch and erase tiny lines forming on his brow as he frowned.

Too bad, he has a partner.

Darn it, the cute ones are gay.

Oh well, she wasn't dating yet anyway. Leo said he'd call, but she hadn't heard from him.

Tray was devilishly handsome and rugged. He was charming in a decisive way and spurred something inside Zoe pushing her toward being ready quicker than Mom's or Casey's sly nudges had. Tray was masculine and fine, oozing testosterone from every pore. His honey smooth voice melted any resistance she had toward the male species. Too bad she was extremely attracted to the guy.

He had a partner. Even if he didn't, he preferred men. She didn't have a chance with him.

On the bright side, renewed interest in the opposite sex was a positive. She'd merely humored Casey with the silly ceremony declaring she was moving on and releasing Hal. Maybe it had actually helped.

Listening carefully to her client, reading between the lines, Chloe tried understanding the meaning behind his comments. She smiled and stood. "Okay, we're done here. You in a hurry, or do you have time to view another property not far away?"

A delightful smile spread across his face making him even better looking and making her curse his sexual preference once more. "I have time. What 'cha got in mind?"

She strode to the entrance and donned her muddy boots, locking doors and flipping off lights as she went. She once again sat on the door lip and stepped into the muddy front yard.

Mr. Ackerson followed doing the same. He held the muddy bag they'd sat their shoes on. She retrieved a second from her tote and slipped the nasty one inside. At her SUV she donned her heels and slipped her boots inside a trash bag. She selected another and handed it to him.

"Here you go, in case you want to place it in your floorboard to keep mud off."

He shook his head dubiously. "Too late I'm afraid. My *beater* has seen worse."

She brought up a photo on her iPad. "This listing sounds more to your liking. We can drive over to take a glance."

He stooped to her height to share her screen, /their shoulders bumped, and he didn't move away. She finger slid pictures across for his perusal. His eyes lit up. Excitement pulsed through his flannel sleeve and her linen dress, sending a thrill to her nether-region. A twinge in her groin was an itch that wasn't about to be scratched.

Whoa, girl. Don't get excited. He's taken.

Standing erect with a broad smile, his head bobbed. "Now this is more like it. It's modern but not stark. It appears smaller than this monstrosity. That means easier management. I'm all for that. What's the price? Is it vacant so we can see it right away?"

"It is, and I made an appointment already in case you wanted to view it tonight. I figured if you wrote an offer on this one, I'd cancel it. It's priced barely less than this one." She pointed to the price on the listing sheet on her screen. "Its five minutes from here. Follow me in your truck.

45

"Great. Let's do it."

She hopped into her SUV waiting for him to climb into his vehicle.

Moments later they entered a contemporary home. "There are five bedrooms, seven baths and a large family and game room occupying twenty acres surrounded by woodland and rolling pasture. It is completed and staged with cozy but modern furniture. The outside deck has an outdoor kitchen area and living space, and the pool has not yet been installed. A small, four-stall barn and white, board fencing surround the pastures." He followed as she led him through the features.

No change of footwear was necessary. Sidewalks were poured and landscaping done. After a lengthy tour where he spent considerable time in the main living areas, they exited the front door.

Chloe's had heart raced throughout the viewing. She had trouble staying calm, hiding joy at realization he was making a solid connection with the place.

"I'd like to make an offer on this property."

Her heart did a flip-flop then settled to a loud thumping in her chest. "Wonderful. Follow me to my office? We can write it up."

"I've a better idea. Did you eat dinner? I'm famished after a long day on the job and skipping lunch. I've heard The Royal Diner serves a delicious meal. Let me buy you a meal while you write the contract. We can celebrate over dessert." He acted like a kid begging for a treat. Excitement clearly reflected in his deep chocolate eyes. Too bad the prospect of breaking bread with her wasn't causing his joy. How could she turn him down—gay or not?

Her belly growled quietly at visions of Sadie's food zipping through her mind. Her hand flew to her flat, empty stomach, and her face burn signaled a blush rising.

"I'd love to. You've heard right. Sadie's diner is the best chow in town. Follow me." She hopped into her ride.

Nourishment wasn't the only thing playing havoc with Chloe's stomach. Sexy Tray Ackerson was about to provide a commission that would allow her to move on with life. Too bad the fine specimen of manhood was wasted on the other sex. Chloe might've gladly spent quality time with the handsome newcomer, if he were into women.

The quick drive gave her time to calm her over-active libido down. It had been a long time since that baby had been satisfied. At least it

CHAPTER 5

The center of Sweetwater housed mostly aging two and three story buildings and small shops joining forces with modern structures completing the busy city center. Five banks could be seen from the entrance to Sadie's Royal Diner. The courthouse and police station crowned the end of the lane where the street circled a small park with an ornate gazebo.

Chloe parked in front of the restaurant then hopped out, tossed a contract packet in her tote and followed Mr. Ackerson to the door. He held it wide, as a gentleman should; and they stepped inside.

Sadie rushed toward Chloe with open arms. The flashy, red-headed waitress, wearing a retro pink and white uniform and white apron with a pen tucked behind an ear, grinned as broad as Sweetwater valley was wide.

"Well, I'll be . . . if it ain't Chloe Roberts. Honey child, I heard you was moving back home and working for your ma. How the heck are ya,' darlin' girl?" Sadie's thick, southern drawl never failed to bring a grin to Chloe's face.

The older woman snuggling Chloe tight then extending her arms for an up-and-down inspection, reminding Chloe how glad she was she'd returned to her hometown, and filling her with warmth of Sadie's generous welcome Folks in Sweetwater appreciated and took care of their own, whether they liked you or not. Sadie liked everyone and had the warmest heart in town.

49

"You heard right. I'm here to stay." Pulling away she straightened and waived Tray's direction. "Sadie, I'd like you to meet my friend and client, Tray Ackerson. Tray is moving to town, and I'm helping him find a home. Tray, Sadie Carson, owner-operator of the Royal Diner and the best cook in town."

Sadie shook Tray's hand joyously. "Thank ya, darlin'. Welcome, Mr. Ackerson. You chose right, picking our Chloe for your agent. I hear tell she's one heck of a businesswoman."

Chloe's face heated at the compliment. New Yorkers never praised her for doing her job well, though she'd been efficient, professional and successful there.

"Thank you, Ms. Carson. I heard the same thing. I have to agree, from what I've seen so far." Tray shook Sadie's hand. Her long, red nails now and slender hand was sprouting age spots—another reminder of time passing since Chloe left town.

"Call me Sadie, young feller. Everybody does. Now ya 'all go on. Pick you a table. I'll bring you some water while ya decide. There's fresh blackberry cobbler for dessert, if you're in the mood and got room for it." She bustled toward the kitchen slower than she had when Chloe was a teenager.

"I'm always in the mood for her cobblers, especially blackberry." Chloe led Tray to an empty table in a corner of the crowded room. She spoke with several people they passed. Customers happily welcomed her home. It was the first time in years she'd seen many of them.

Handing Tray a folder from the table, she chose a contract packet from her bag. "While you peruse this, I'll start the paperwork. I know the menu by heart. You're in for a treat." She enjoyed anticipation in his soulful eyes.

Too bad super cute ones were always gay.

"You know everyone in town." He looked impressed—a big-city guy amused at small-town fellowship.

"It's a tight-knit community. Everyone knows everyone else's business. Prepare yourself. It's nothing like New York." She winked and began writing. "Are you sure you don't want your partner to view the property before signing the offer?"

"No, it's not necessary. He couldn't care less, but I can't wait to show him the great room tile. You've got to find out who laid it for me. I have jobs lined up and want to hire the contractor to do them."

"I'm sure the seller will happily recommend his vendor, when I tell him how pleased you are."

"The artistic design is stylish and unique. He must've done the master bath as well. It's a work of art."

"Yes. The tub and shower are enormous. A whole family could fit in there." It should work well for her tall, handsome client and his partner, no matter how large the partner was.

Tray provided details to insert into the forms as she wrote. Sadie arrived to take their orders. By the time meals were served a substantial offer was ready for presenting. Chloe pocketed the contract in her tote then paid attention to her dinner and companion.

The evening's sunny rays before sunset made Tray's dark mane appear almost blue-black. Expressive eyes revealed a joyful disposition as they chatted, and he acted elated and anxious to get the property deal accepted. He was an entertaining companion, making cute jokes and acting like he was thoroughly enjoying himself.

"Will the house be a base to work from and somewhere to sleep besides hotels? Or do you plan to make Sweetwater your home?" She couldn't curb her curiosity.

"That depends on how successful my subdivision is. Let's hope the first phase goes well, and I can make Sweetwater a long-term proposition."

"I should receive an answer by tomorrow night. I'll call soon as I hear from the seller." She took another bite of her burger. Delightful flavors melted in her mouth, and she resisted moaning in delight.

"Awesome. I'm chomping at the bit to get an answer. I can't believe how anxious I feel. It's not like me to put so much of myself into a business decision. It surprises me how much I adored the house. You knew exactly what I needed. I haven't had a real home in years. I look forward to settling down and having a place of my own." Vulnerability in his thick, strong voice added a special charm she hadn't witnessed before. This all-business entrepreneur put his heart into this decision.

"Meeting new people is my favorite part of the job. Assisting folks like you and your partner to find the perfect location is what I do." She was confidant his bid would work out, but didn't want to get his hopes up. She'd done a good job for Tray and advised him on pricing, but rarely did a client buy her a meal. "Thank you for dinner. I hadn't realized how hungry I was until you mentioned food." She dipped a crispy fry in a pile of ketchup on her plate.

He eyed her oddly. "You're welcome. I wanted try this place and couldn't face eating alone. I do it way too often. I'm glad you were free."

Business travel must keep the poor man sadly separated from his partner. Good thing she'd accepted his invitation. It was the least she could do.

He bit into a slice of meatloaf, following it with a sizable forkful of fluffy, buttery mashed potatoes, carrots and peas. "Sadie's reputation stands—delicious. I'm sick of rubber chicken business dinners, steak houses and eating takeout at home."

"Don't you or your partner cook? You barely gave a cursory glance at the kitchens of both houses." It would be a waste not using that glorious workspace.

He acted perplexed. "I enjoy cooking when I have an afternoon to indulge in it. I work so much, I rarely have the luxury. It's not worth the effort to cook for one. I think he cooks; I'm not sure. Why?"

She cocked her head. "Oh, have you just been together a short while?" *New lovers?* It would explain why Tray missed him so.

"Five years, but it never came up. We rarely discuss such things."

That seemed odd. "He doesn't live with you?"

More confusion crossed his face. Then he broke into a wicked grin. "No, he lives with his wife." He wagged his brows, catching on.

Blood gushed to her face, and it burned with embarrassment. Boy, did she trip over her tongue.

"I see. I'm sorry. I didn't mean to appear nosy."

"It's okay. I understand. You think I'm gay. Right?" Tray's good-natured chuckle showed he found her mistake humorous.

Her brows shot up as she laid her burger down and placed her hands beside her plate. "Seriously? You're not?"

Great. She looked like an idiot in front of her first client. *Way to go, Chloe.*

"Absolutely, one-hundred-percent heterosexual here— so is my partner, far as I know. At least his family thinks so. We're business associates, not lovers. We work together. That's all. Don't feel bad. From our conversation earlier, I see how you came to the conclusion." Humor filtered his explanation, and his shoulders jiggled as he talked. He was getting a chuckle out of her faux pas. Rightfully so.

"Damn. I'm a fool. I'm so sorry if I've made you uncomfortable. Upsetting you was not my intention."

53

He guffawed and held her hand in his. Heat bathed her skin, sizzling blood and seeping through an arm to her chest causing her to force air into her lungs.

Her eyes couldn't help gazing at his perfectly manicured nails and contradicting manner of dress. The construction worker outfit did not define him. This man didn't do manual labor. The heaviest tools he handled were likely a flashlight and set of plans. Tray was obviously accustomed to being in charge. The powerful man was sexy as hell—and not gay.

Yippee!

He eyed his nails. The recent shiny coat of clear enamel sent a last snicker out of him laughing at himself, instead of her.

Good.

"Nope, I'm not embarrassed. I'm amused. Our talk about design, art, decorating, my fancy fingernails and mention of a partner were misleading. I understand how you got the wrong impression." His delighted expression proved he was sincere.

"Well." Pulling her hand from his grasp casually, she winced. "Good, I'm humiliated enough for both of us." She shook her head glancing at the ceiling.

"Don't be. At least it's out of the way before I make a proposition."

Oh hell no. Proposition? She tried to maintain a semblance of dignity. If this guy thought she'd make up for her mistake by sleeping with him, he had another thing coming. She found him attractive but didn't sleep with clients. Maybe after the closing, when they knew each other better and had no business contact—if he played his cards right.

Tray seemed to be studying her, as though weighing options. If he was judging her character based on the last few minutes, she wasn't interested in him after all. Surely he wasn't pissed.

Finally he tented his hands together on the table and cleared his throat. His voice returned to the business-like manner she'd heard when he'd contacted her on the phone. "I'm developing a large plot of land at the edge of town. It includes single family, one and two-story houses, and a section of luxury condos. I want you to act as my listing agent. I like the way you handle yourself. You're a pro."

He could've knocked her over with a good exhale. She blinked, still open mouthed, not believing her luck. "That's awesome."

"Great. Section one has twenty-five homes and twenty-five condos. I'll meet you at your office tomorrow morning at nine to go over the plans, time line, cost basis and models."

"Fine." He didn't ask, but assumed she wasn't booked. She wasn't, but it would've been nice if he had inquired. He was definitely boss man material—and he was her new boss.

What was more thrilling—getting the listings on his business or learning he was single and into women? Maybe both.

Hoody-hoo, not bad for my first day—a fabulous sale and fifty listings with more to come.

CHAPTER 6

Tray met Chloe as planned. They spent a better part of the morning boning up on his properties, talking price, square footage, options and contracts before he finally left for a job site. She finished the day ensuring his homes were properly input into the Multiple Listing System and engaged the marketing plan they agreed to.

Stopping by her desk, Ava smiled at her busy daughter. "My goodness, Chloe, you're having an exceptionally successful beginning for your career in Sweetwater. I'm excited and thrilled for you. Can I buy you dinner to celebrate?" Ava preened, proud as a mare watching her foal take her first steps.

"Thanks, Mom. Having your support means a lot. I'd love to go with you, but Casey and I are touring houses tonight. I listed Tray's subdivision, so that should be lucrative. I'm closing on his purchase Tuesday. Combined with equity from selling the New York condo, my income is sufficient to purchase a place here."

"I'd agree, but don't move too fast. You're comfortable living with Casey. What's the hurry?" It was understandable Ava was hesitant to see her daughter as a grown up. After living away, returning to the nest would spur old habits. Fear of falling into those childhood behaviors was one reason she'd avoided living with her mom when she'd returned. Chloe didn't want to get off to a bad start.

"Casey is the best, and she's more than hospitable. I'm used to having my own space and am anxious to settle down." She needed her independence. It had been years since she'd allowed Ava to hover over her. It was enough she'd leaned on Casey until now. It was time. Ava would get used to it.

"All right, sweetie. Show me what you found. I might know of other suitable properties." She leaned across Chloe's shoulder.

Chloe pulled up visuals of the houses she had carefully selected on her laptop. "What do you think?" Chloe printed listing sheets.

"You've done a good job choosing. I'd say this about does it, but there's one on Douglas you might also consider." Taking the keyboard Ava selected an address, and another property popped onto the screen. "What do you think of this one?"

"Thanks, Mom. I know the one. It is cramped; and it's farther from the office, from you and Gran and also from Casey. I'll keep it in mind if none of these is suitable. We've got enough to see tonight and want to check them out before going to dinner. We're trying the new Irish Pub. I hear they have a great fish basket." She shut her computer.

Bending to kiss her daughter's forehead, Ava smiled. "They do indeed. It sounds like you've got it under control. Happy hunting." Ava headed toward her office then turned around. "I figured by now you'd have a date scheduled with Leo. Or maybe Tray might ask you out. You need to start dating, Chloe." She leaned against a wall crossing her legs.

"No worries, Mom. Tray is interesting and charming, but he's my client. Leo called earlier and asked me to dinner tomorrow night. We're going to the French bistro on Main. Rest assured; I don't need you to manage my love life."

Ava stood erect and chuckled. "Sorry, I don't want to become a meddling mom. You're an adult. I can't help my concern, however. Bear with me, darling. I'm trying to stay out of your affairs."

"No problem, Mom. I get it. I love you." She blew Ava a kiss.

Ava puckered returning the affection before entering her glass-walled office. She grabbed her purse then waved and smiled as she exited the building.

♥♥♥♥

Chloe and Casey arrived at their first location. "Tell me about the dude you sold the fancy house to. Is he cute? Nice? Did you like him?"

"Tray Ackerson is a developer moving to Sweetwater and has a large residential subdivision in the works. He's gorgeous, well-built and apparently has money to burn—and yes. I liked him fine. I embarrassed myself to death. I got the impression he was gay and kept chattering about his partner. He wasn't offended, but thought it was funny."

Casey guffawed. "That's hilarious. It's good he's got a sense of humor."

"He's got more than that. He's the best looking thing I've seen in forever. Think Marlboro Man mixed with Nick Clooney and Tom Cruise. If he weren't dressed like a construction worker, he could've stepped out of Esquire Magazine." She hopped from the vehicle.

"What about Leo? You two hit it off at the bowling alley the other night."

"Yes. We did. I liked him more than a little. Leo seems like a wonderful guy. I'm anxious to get to know him. He called earlier, and we're going out tomorrow. You sure it's okay?" She studied Casey's face. She wouldn't hurt her friend for anything. Her belly tingled when Leo came up, and she liked emotions his attention spurred, but if Casey wanted, she'd break the date.

"It's more than okay. It's great. I hoped the two of you would connect. Leo's fabulous, but he hasn't seen anyone seriously in a long time."

"We'll see how it goes. I'm looking forward to it." Chloe sighed with relief at Casey's blessing.

"This house shows decently from the outside. Let's check it out." Casey started for the front door with Chloe tagging behind.

"The owner is home." Chloe said ringing the doorbell. The agent said the older woman is disabled, and it's inconvenient for her to leave. The people living with her won't be home."

"Come in." A raspy voice rang through the door after the chimes stopped.

Chloe opened it, and they stepped in. She glanced at Casey. They wrinkled their noses. "Wonder what?" Chloe mouthed the words.

Casey shrugged, and they entered the unpleasant smelling house with trepidation.

Tidy, worn furnishings filled the area. A few toys tucked here and there. Poor lighting didn't help. Window blinds were pulled shut giving the house a dark, gloomy atmosphere.

A television blasted from the living room. An old woman hooked to an oxygen producing machine, sat in a worn lounge chair watching news.

"Hi, you must be the owner. I'm Chloe Roberts; and this is my friend, Casey Martin. I'm the agent and prospective buyer. Casey is here to help. Thanks for allowing us to view your home today."

"No problem. Go about your showing. I'm here if you need me. Don't go in the front room upstairs. It's the same as the other one, but it's blue. Rhonda had babies, and she's in there. Don't disturb her." Her raspy voice growled as pleasantly as it seemed she could manage gasping for air.

Taken aback, Chloe didn't know how to respond. "Oh, okay. Thanks." She shrugged to Casey then led her up the staircase.

The bedroom was large, but needed painting. A mattress lay on the floor. Wrinkled clothing was strewn about in massive disarray. The smell was less pervasive on the second floor, but was still rank. She couldn't figure it out. Her brows arched glancing at the chipped paint on the door across the hallway before trotting downstairs.

A quick run through the kitchen proved it large and in need of updating. The single bath was long and narrow with older fixtures and broken tiles. Nearing the hallway door she turned to the owner. "Is this the basement?" The stench was stronger here.

Ugh. Probably not worth checking.

"Yep, go on down. Sampson won't bother you, long as you leave him alone." She didn't look up from watching television.

Dubiously, Chloe eyed Casey who shrugged rolling her eyes. "Okay, thanks." Foul odor grew stronger nearing the entrance. Easing it wider steadily, Chloe glanced into a dark stairway of a disgusting scented basement, almost knocking her blind as the door opened. She flipped the light switch, mentally noting to use hand sanitizer when she left. The floor was marred with piles of nasty brown. She flipped lights off and shut the door securely trying not to slam it.

"It's okay. We've seen enough. We'll skip the basement."

The old gal shrugged. "Suit yourself."

Casey cocked her head eying the owner. "I'm curious. What kind of critter is Sampson, and is Rhonda animal or human?"

"They're boa constrictors." Again, she didn't bother glancing at them.

"Oh—" was all Chloe was capable of saying. She didn't waste time bolting for the exit. Whipping it open she shouted behind her. "Thanks for allowing the showing."

Casey sped out hot on her footsteps. She secured the door behind them and gazed at Chloe with her face screwed up and mouth open. "Yew." She spat the word. Casey and Chloe shivered and danced around on the sidewalk taking huge gulps of fresh air.

"Yuck, ick, ohhh . . ." Chloe quivered all the way to her car.

Casey started giggling and couldn't stop. Chloe joined as they jumped into the SUV. "Let's get the hell out of here. Disgusting." She shivered and squinted.

Chloe winced. "Snakes, and they don't clean up after them. Can you imagine? It was the most sickening thing I've run into during my career as a real estate agent—and I've seen some mighty disturbing properties." She gasped at untainted oxygen.

"I've never smelled such horrific stench in my life." Casey closed her eyes shaking her head.

"On to the next listing."

Chloe used her electronic key to enter the vacant house. After walking through the one-story property, she paused in the galley kitchen. "The rooms are freshly painted, and there's new carpeting. The bathroom is tiny, and this kitchen is not for me. This place is too cramped."

"I agree. I can't see you living here. There's no yard to speak of and not even a place to sit outside."

They hopped into Chloe's vehicle and drove a short distance to a lovely tree-lined neighborhood.

"I'm excited to see this one. I prefer a one-story." Chloe knocked on the door. "Someone lives here, but he shouldn't be home. I'll make sure before barging in. I've surprised my share of sleeping and naked people." She chuckled. When no answer came, she unlocked the lock box and used the key.

The bright, sunny, sparsely furnished living room with windows on two sides had hardwood flooring spotted with throw rugs in strategic locations. An archway led into a sizable dining area housing a card table and chairs. A stack of mail and newspapers occupied the kitchen counter top.

"Great appliances—they're fairly new and appear barely used." Chloe opened the range and glanced inside. "The freezer and side-by-side refrigerator are clean. The kitchen is large enough to accommodate a small table set and barstools at the island."

Casey leaned on the counter. "Look, Chloe; the soapstone sink overlooks the back yard and covered porch spanning the back of the house. One end has a swing, and there's a picnic table at the other. The yard is level, and there's privacy from trees and a fence."

"It's beautiful. I love the large shade tree. I could keep a mower and tools in that nice storage shed." She was getting a great vibe from the house, filling her with anticipation and excitement.

"Yep, and your bike will fit in there."

Chloe opened a door. "Look, there's a sizable pantry."

Casey wandered down a short hallway. "The bath is nice with retro tile."

"Not a problem. I like the older, small blocks. Black and white lends itself to being lovely when decorated properly. I could do a lot with the bath."

Opening another door revealed a small bedroom filled with cartons. "The seller is apparently preparing for his move. Not bad for a second bedroom. Hopefully the master is larger."

Casey opened the second door to a large bedroom with sparse furniture. Men's clothing lay haphazardly about an unmade bed. Chloe opened a door discovering a messy walk-in closet. "This could accommodate my things well. The room is plenty big enough—so good, so far." Anticipation mounted.

Casey stepped to the last door which stood open at the far corner of the room. Blood drained from her face. Her jaws went limp. She whitened like billowy clouds that dotted a blue sky, and her mouth hung open. She appeared ready to pass out.

Confused, Chloe rushed closer anxious to see and catch her wilting buddy.

She froze.

A small bath retro-tiled bath in identical black and white as the half-bath, was splattered red. A man lay halfway in the walk-in shower stall. His blank eyes stared lifelessly.

Chloe backed away pulling Casey with her. They ran to the front door and outside. As they neared her vehicle Chloe yanked her phone from her purse and hit nine-one-one. An operator asked her location. She receipted the address with a quivering voice.

"There's a dead man in the shower of a house with blood everywhere. We escaped to the front yard. Yes, it's for sale. We had an appointment to view it. No, I don't believe so. We didn't hear anyone in the property. Yes, he's dead. There's too much blood for him to be alive, and he appears to have been there awhile." Trembling speech amplified her already frightened state, and her body began to quake.

Casey bent over with hands on knees trying not to hyperventilate by taking deep breaths and counting slowly. Chloe placed a hand on her back. Her mind raced, and her head buzzed.

"Yes, we'll wait in the drive. Thank you."

CHAPTER 7

A cruiser whipped into the driveway and parked behind Chloe's vehicle, blocking her leave. Not that she had the ability to drive anyway. Chloe and Casey shook like bobble-head dolls on game day holding each other up, and they weren't going anywhere.

A six-foot uniformed deputy peeled his long limbs from the automobile wearing a rueful expression. Rising to his full stature, Leo slid his officer's cap over sandy, blonde hair.

Another cruiser pulled to the curb beside the drive. A glossy, thick mane of silver locks shone in fading spring sunshine as Sheriff Wyatt Gordon stepped out.

Jaiden's curly hair looked forced at gun-point into a tight bun in back, as she climbed from the passenger side. Tawny skin and high cheekbones hinted at her exotic heritage. She grimaced sadly and saluted them.

Leo approached with concern on his handsome face. Chloe figured he'd be more comfortable in a tee shirt and shorts, but she did like a guy in a well-fitted uniform.

"Holy crap, Casey, Chloe—you made the call? You discovered the body?" His arms went forward then limp at his sides, like he longed to cradle the distraught women but thought better of it. Fumbling with his hands, he paced a couple steps. Then he spun. Lifting his hat, a hand slid across his hair before securing it in place. He glared with his mouth opened then glanced toward his boss and back at them.

Jaiden had sidled to stand beside him. "You gals okay?" Concern filtered from her dark eyes, and she placed a hand on Chloe and Casey's arms in a tender gesture making Chloe feel safer.

Chloe's quivering voice answered with a nod. "Yes. You know I'm a real estate agent searching for a home to purchase myself. Casey came along to help Our third and final stop we toured the house except for the basement and found a body in the master bathroom."

Casey shivered clinging to Chloe's arm. "There's blood everywhere. His eyes are open, but he's definitely dead. I touched his ankle. The body is cold. I . . . I . . . didn't disturb anything." Chloe's arm slipped around her shoulders.

"No, we tried not to bother anything after we found him. Our prints are all over the house, but we didn't realize a crime had been committed when we got here." Chloe wished Leo would touch her or do something to make a personal connection. His business-like attitude was probably to be expected, but it put her on edge and made her sad.

He looked nervous. "How did you know it was a crime?"

Chloe moaned. "He's a mess. It appears he was beat to death."

"Wow, okay, definitely a crime scene." He shuffled back and forth and gave Chloe a sympathetic, closed-mouth smile. "I'm heading up the investigation, meaning we need to postpone plans for tomorrow night. Even if we clear the two of you before then, I'll be working long hours until the case is solved."

She nodded with a sigh, not having considered being suspected in the crime.

The sheriff neared. "Wyatt, I'm glad you're here." Chloe hadn't come in contact with Sheriff Wyatt Gordon since returning home, but she'd known him her whole life.

"Sorry this is under dire circumstances." Wyatt drawled in his slow, southern style. He might be old as her dad, but he was a looker, even with his full head of prematurely silver hair.

Leo took charge. "Okay, ladies, I'm asking you to sit in your vehicle. Jaiden will take your statements while Sheriff Gordon and I check the house."

Wyatt gave them a concerned visual appraisal then smiled calmly. "You gals are fine. No worries. Go with Jaiden. Let us take care of this. I'll oversee the case, but Leo is taking point. Want me to contact someone for you—your mom's?"

"*Noooo . . . please* don't call Mom. Let me tell her." Chloe whined.

The natural protector's face filled with concern. Sweetwater was lucky he'd returned from Chicago to take the sheriff's job. His charming, laid-back, easy-going, gentlemanly way with words and actions calmed a person in crisis. His presence assured Chloe all would be fine.

Wyatt approached with arms wide. Both women slid into the hug and cried heartily against his broad shoulders.

Would she ever forget the sight?

"The blood—" she muttered, unaware she was speaking until she recognized the voice.

"I'd heard you moved home, Chloe. A right depressing howdy-do—if you ask me. Welcome home, sweetheart. Don't worry, you'll get through this unscathed."

"Thanks, Wyatt. I'm glad you're here."

"I'm involved from start-to-finish but didn't want to lead because Ava and I have been buddies since we could walk. Officer Sanders is capable, and it's his case. You're in good hands. Go with Jaiden now, and give your statement." His confident manner and twang were comforting.

"Wyatt, we're friends with Jaiden and Leo, too." Casey eyed the sheriff.

"I realize that. But I've known the two of you longer. It's a small force—hard finding anyone who doesn't know folks around here. It's fine. We can handle it." He peeled them off and strolled toward the door.

Leo's flat tummy rose and fell showing signs he wasn't happy with the situation. His shoulders rose, and he turned toward the house.

She'd pictured the soft-spoken deputy's slender frame on a running track or working out with weights. Biceps like his didn't come naturally. It was sexy when men took care of themselves. Her hankering to see Leo after a sweltering, sweaty run, with taunt, brimming muscles pressing veins to the surface, was squelched by his tight, uniformed butt striding away.

Way to distract me, Leo.

Oddly, she was thinking about stripping Leo bare at such a time. Her newly awakening libido had a mind of its own. Oh well, she couldn't help the dead guy, but Leo could do wonders for her. Her longing for the would have to wait until he wasn't distracted.

She sighed, feeling light-headed and suddenly heavy. Her shoulders slumped, and she closed her eyes for a second, pursing her lips.

Jaiden slipped an arm around their shoulders ushering them toward Chloe's vehicle. "Come on. Let's get you to the car. You need to sit." Nodding, they blindly obeyed, grateful for her take-charge attitude.

Hal's handsome face flashed through Chloe's mind. He'd acted remorseful and resolved the day he left for a run after their blowout, giving her time to cool down before saying things they couldn't take back. It was the last anyone saw of Hal Spence. She never got to ogle him, sweaty and oozing sex appeal, trying to coax forgiveness out of her.

Shaking off the apparition, Chloe brought her mind to present. She had enough to deal with in the here-and-now. No time for revelations about the past or prophesy of unhappiness. She'd put the Hal situation to rest. It needed to stay there.

Another siren blared, and an EMT unit parked behind Wyatt's cruiser. A dark sedan came to a stop behind it. A squirrelly, short man with a paunch stepped out. A ring of thinning hair spanned from ear-to-ear crowned by a shiny scalp, and he wore thick glasses. He approached Wyatt carrying a clipboard. Chloe figured him for the coroner. A third cruiser pulled to the curb. A couple officers emerged carrying duffel bags marked *CSI.* They began cordoning the site with yellow ribbon.

Jaiden slipped into the back seat. Chloe and Casey took the front. "Sorry, you stepped into this. You look pale. Are you alright?" Jaiden patted their shoulders from behind.

"It's good having familiar faces in charge. It helps me resist the urge to flee." It wasn't so when Hal disappeared. She was the prime suspect of foul play, and NYPD had treated her abruptly. "I can't wait to get out of here." Chloe admitted.

"That's a natural instinct, even from an innocent person. We'll make this as quick as possible." Jaiden asked detailed questions and typed notes on an iPad. She was considerate and professional. Sympathy radiated from her for the two women shocked out of their socks.

71

Chloe wiped beads of sweat from above her lips and answered Jaiden's questions as best she could. Casey stuttered unlike herself and tremors marred her normal confident speech.

After what felt like hours, Jaiden laid her device aside and smiled. "What did you gals think of the house?"

Casey snorted with her hands tucked under her arms. "There was a dead guy in it. It's enough to scare me off."

Chloe's hands felt clammy. She glanced skyward to the left pursing her lips then met her friend's eyes. "I don't know, Casey. I liked the house. Location is perfect. It has everything I need and is priced right. I'll bet the owner will be eager to negotiate because of the murder stigma. He or she will be lucky to sell the place."

Jaiden laughed out loud. "I admire your practicality. You're very much the consummate businesswoman, like your mother." Jaiden's Texas accent sounded similar to a native Kentucky drawl.

"You know Mom?" Chloe's hand flew to her chest.

"Who doesn't? In the few years I've lived in Sweetwater, Ava opened her agency and made a roaring success of it. She's the best broker in town, and she's active in many civic causes."

Pride rushed through Chloe's veins. Her chin rose, thrilled at Jaiden's observation. "Thanks. I don't mind being compared to Mom. She sometimes smothers and constantly pushes me outside my comfort zone; but I dearly love her and respect her. It's not been easy, but Mom's always there for me."

"Ava's one fine lady. I've got all I need. I guess you gals can get going. I'll move Sander's vehicle so you can pull out. We'll be working here a number of hours yet." Jaiden hopped from Chloe's auto.

"I wish you could go with us, Jaiden? Chloe and I were going to dinner, but I'd rather go to the Ten Mile House for a brew. I couldn't swallow a bite, but I could use a drink."

Surprise widened Casey's eyes before they squeezed a tight blink. "You still want to go? Shouldn't we go home?" Casey stuttered then shrugged. She touched her throat then barked a laugh. "On second thought, it's too quiet there. The bar should be filled with people and noise—exactly what we need."

Chloe shrugged and gave her pal a half grin.

Jaiden glanced at the crime scene and back at her friends. "I'd love to join you gals. If your car is still at the tavern when I get off, I'll stop by. Don't count on me. I'll be here awhile."

"Understood. I'm not anxious to go to bed. I doubt I'll sleep at all. Hopefully we'll you later." Chloe waved.

Jaiden walked toward the cruiser. After the deputy moved it out of the way, she backed out of the drive.

The girls were unusually quiet as Chloe drove toward town center. Chloe's skin tingled recalling the scene. She needed chatter to distract her from what they'd witnessed. "Jaiden acts like an experienced law-dog."

"Yep; she was injured in a drug bust when she was a Texas Ranger. Her brother, Calvin, a retired Navy Seals, moved to Sweetwater. Their dad had recently died; and their mom, Brightleaf Coldwater, had retired her vet practice to join him. When Jaiden was hurt, she came here to recoup with family."

"Is Cal anywhere as good looking as his sister?" Her breath still caught as she spoke, a lingering effect of trauma, no doubt.

Casey's eyes rolled and smiled as she nodded. "He's a hunk—dark, sweltering sex appeal wrapped into a tall, muscular frame simply oozing testosterone—extremely happy on the eyes. Wait until you see him."

"Really? So why haven't you been after the guy?" Chloe chuckled, relieved to discuss anything besides earlier events.

"No such luck. Unfortunately he's taken. Cal fell immediately for Rose Casson, Sage's farmhand at Parsley, Sage, Rose, Mary & Wine. I mentioned Sage, Wyatt's wife, to you earlier."

"Yeah, I remember. She's the hippie. Right?"

Casey nodded. "Anyway soon as Cal saw Rose, he flipped. Before we knew it, they were married."

"And Jaiden is engaged to a doctor?"

"Yeah; last year Clay Barnes returned to town. She calls him Doc. They've been together ever since. Clay is a surgeon at the hospital where I work, and he's partners in a practice in town."

"When I went away to school, Wyatt had married and moved to Chicago. I figured Wyatt's buddy Levi for a lifelong bachelor, but I hear he's married also. Funny how things change." She'd missed a lot while away. Life kept moving, whether you saw it or not.

Casey snickered. "Yep, everyone thought so, including Levi. He met Sage's friend, Riley Powers, an ad gal with an agency in Cincinnati. After a rocky romance, they tied the knot in a double wedding with Levi's sister, Corrie and Justin Henderson, who owns the Ten Mile House we're headed to."

"Damn, I've missed the gossip. When I attended college, Corrie was CFO of their family business and married to some hotshot fashion photographer in New York. I think they had a little girl. Justin was hitched to a horse trainer who worked for Levi. I can't remember her name, but Mom mentioned they had a baby."

"Everyone figured Justin was going to kill himself when he fell off the deep end after Becky and Bonnie tragically died, drinking and carousing like a wild man. Corrie divorced her cheating husband and returned with their teenage daughter, Morgan. A couple years later, Corrie and Justin got together. I guess they helped each other recover. She's still the Adelle Corporation CEO, but commutes to New York as needed."

"Justin's a super guy. Didn't he have an accident when he was younger?"

"Yes; he lost a leg in a motorcycle accident. His limp is barely detectable, unless he's tired. He'll likely be tending bar tonight. "

"It's good catching up with everyone. We're younger than their crowd, but they're wonderful people. I love everything about this town—except . . . the dead guy in my shower." She snickered, picturing her belongings throughout the cottage.

"Seriously? You're actually considering the house?" Casey eyed her with mouth open. She gazed away chuckling. "I should have known, you'd push emotion from the equation and make a fact-based decision."

Chloe's racing heartbeat slowed, and breathlessness subsided as she parked. "You know me well, Casey. I love you, babe."

CHAPTER 8

Several hours later, Jaiden strolled into the hopping Ten Mile House to the tune of a Creedence song on the juke box. She'd changed from her uniform into tight-fitting jeans and a tank top. Four inch-heeled boots tapped wood flooring as she spoke with friends and neighbors, strolling toward Chloe and Casey's table along a wall. She waved at Justin, serving brews at the long bar.

"Glad you made it. We're way ahead of you." Chloe pointed to the spare chair at their table. She was glad her new friend had been able to join.

"Thanks." She yanked a seat out. "I got out earlier than I thought. The team assumed the bulk of the work. I guess they'll pull me more into it tomorrow. But that's another day." She patted Casey's hand. Giving Jaiden a close-mouthed smile, Casey gripped her hand.

"Who was the man? Can you share that much?" Curiosity was itching at Chloe, and she wanted to weigh the odds to come up with a game plan for negotiating a purchase.

"Sure. He was the homeowner, Harvey Carnes. Apparently it's a divorce case. The wife already moved out. He was staying there while trying to sell." Deputy Jaiden Coldwater took a seat at her friends' table.

Casey released her grip on her friend and leaned on elbows nursing a sweating, amber bottle. "Know anything about him?"

"Not much; he worked at a Lexington supply company called Foundation Enterprises, based out of New York. They provide equipment, labor and supplies for construction. I think he was a number cruncher, office drone type—nothing elaborately important—not a top decision-maker."

Jaiden shrugged accepting the beer Justin Henderson placed in front of her. He obviously knew what she'd order. Checking their table ensuring the others had full drinks he smiled, nodded then left them alone. He was still handsome in a short, tightly wound, brooding manner and barely limped on his prosthesis, wearing a boot matching the one on his actual foot. If she hadn't known, no way could she tell he had one single leg.

A slender, drunken female with purplish-red, cropped hair; tight jeans and low-cut top stumbled against her barstool. Obviously having partaken of one too many, she leaned on a girlfriend sitting beside her.

"A news bulletin I heard on my way here said the boy whore I was sleeping with was murdered. Someone did old Harvey in. It had to be his bitch wife. Helen Carnes is a devil. The fruitcake punctured my tires. I found my car that way the morning after she and I had it out. No doubt she did it. Now this—she killed Harvey." Her words slurred loud enough the tavern crowd heard causing a buzz immediately sounding around the room. Several people checked their cell phones while others whispered to each other.

Adrenalin pulsed through Chloe. The drunkard's friend braced an arm around her and ushered the teetering female out. Patrons appeared relieved, some smiling as they chattered among themselves. The Sweetwater grapevine was hard at work, and Chloe had yet to tell Ava.

"Who was the gal?" Chloe turned to Casey and Jaiden.

Casey shrugged. Jaiden snickered. "My first interrogation tomorrow; hopefully she sleeps it off. I'm going to have a chat with Sandy Bennet when she sobers. She knows something." One brow rose, and Jaiden bit the side of her lip.

"She's the dead dude's girlfriend. Maybe she did it." Chloe's guts twitched.

"You'll interrogate the wife too. Right?" Casey's eyes spanned wide, and she stammered.

"You bet. Helen Carnes is top of the list. One of us will speak with her. Wyatt's probably already doing it. He had to notify her, as next of kin."

A tall blonde with long, sleek tresses sauntered to the table and leaned against an empty chair smelling of whiskey and brimstone. Her boobs threatened to pop out of the top button of her tight shirt.

"I'll be damned if it ain't Chloe Roberts come back to haunt the town. How long you staying, bitch? We'll take a relieved breath, once you're gone again." Her ample knockers stuck out further, and she rested a hand on a rounded hip.

Jaiden almost spit a gulp of beer suppressing laughter. Casey's face grew stern, and her mouth crimped confining fumes appearing ready to gush from her. She released a loud sigh, but didn't speak.

Chloe pushed a hefty sigh out. "Lucky you and lucky Sweetwater—I've moved home to stay. It's nice of you to welcome me home, Stacy. Are you still running the local coven? Who've you bewitched lately?" Chloe's words flowed soft and even-tempered. She wasn't about to let the alcohol-fueled witch get to her, like she had too many times in high school.

"Not your business, but I married your old flame, Carl Townsend. I figured your ma would've broken news to you years ago. Poor Carl finally found a woman who could satisfy him. We've got two little ones. I hear tell you can't hang on to a man, much less have a family." Stacy wobbled uneasily with her arm swaying.

Ouch, that stung.

Ava had shared the Townsend's good news. Carl was the last person Chloe wanted, but she'd assumed she'd have kids by now. Her maternal clock ticked away ripe for kicking; and her tormentor had perfected the tyrant act long ago.

I'll be damned if Stacy will know she struck a nerve.

She took a slow easy breath, and kept her expression cordial. "My condolences to your husband. If you by some long-shot make him happy, more power to you. Carl Townsend is a decent guy and deserves happiness, even if he wasn't the man for me."

"Obviously; you tossed him aside for a big city education and career. Guess that was a bust. You've come home with your tail between your legs, licking injured paws. Poor baby, you got what you deserved." Stacy pursed her lips. Chloe's eye twitched, as she resisted the urge to plow into them with her fist.

"Stacy, we're having a private conversation. Feel free to leave." Casey glared slamming hands on the table. Fury must've outweighed her frustration, since it was the most energy she'd expended since they'd arrived.

Jaiden shot to her feet scowling the nasty female in the eye, thanks to spiky footwear. "You got it out of your system, sister. Beat it."

With a *humpf* and haughty shrug, Stacy pranced indignantly to her table, grabbed a purse off a seat and prodded through the crowded bar like a runaway stallion. The door slammed shut behind her.

Jaiden guffawed and slapped her tight-fitted jean-clad leg. "Old nemesis? Everyone's got one. Yours is a real prize." She plopped into her seat.

"Yep, we're polar opposites. I wasn't a good fit for old Carl." Chloe expelled a relieved gush of air.

"Guess he met his match." Jaiden took a sip.

Chloe burst into laughter.

"I'll drink to that." Casey lifted her bottle, and the others tapped theirs together in a toast.

CHAPTER 9

Chloe's doorbell rang. She slipped on shoes as she moved toward the door and whipped it open without looking out. "Hey, Mom. Come in. I'm almost ready for work."

"Chloe, darling, check before opening your door. I could've been an ax murderer." Ava stepped indoors carrying a tray with three coffees, containers of yogurt, fruit and granola.

"Or someone much worse." Chloe glared down her nose with a brow cocked.

"Very funny. I brought breakfast. Is Casey home?"

"Sorry, you missed her. She had an early patient." Chloe stored a yogurt cup in the frig and sipped one of the coffees.

"No problem." Ava selected coffee and a yogurt. She stepped to the drawer and pulled out spoons and napkins. Taking a seat at the island, she began eating and eyed her daughter with an expectant expression.

Chloe shrugged and sat beside her. "Thanks, Mom— very thoughtful." She blew Ava a kiss.

"It's the least I can do." She studied her daughter with a brow cocked.

"You know?"

"It was on the news first thing today, and I've received two calls from friends about it. Why didn't you tell me?"

"I should have known I couldn't beat the Sweetwater gossip train. If you must know, I couldn't bear you gushing around like I'm a fragile piece of china." She didn't meet Ava's glare.

They focused on food for a few minutes. Ava sat her cup down and met her daughter's gaze. "I do not gush. I get carried away sometimes. You're my only daughter, and I love you. You must admit, the circumstances you've fallen into over the last year are far from normal. If anything happened to you it would devastate me."

"So, it's all about you?" She eyed her mom comically. Ava was right, but didn't need Chloe to confirm it.

Shrugging snobbishly Ava winced. "Isn't everything?" They laughed, and it was like old times. Chloe enjoyed bantering giddily with Ava; their way of relieving tension long as Chloe could remember.

Standing, Chloe hugged her mother. "I love you, Mom; and I appreciate everything you do for me. I'd be lost without you."

"Spill." Ava gave her full attention.

"Casey and I were at our last stop. The house was adorable, just what I need. Anyway, the owner was lying on the floor when we inspected the master suite. Blood was everywhere. It was gross. We could see he was dead and ran outside to call the police. Wyatt, Jaiden and Leo showed up first. Then the rest of the crew filed in. Wyatt was wonderful, and offered to call you, but it was too soon. I didn't want you involved at the time. Jaiden questioned Casey and me and let us go before going inside to help with the investigation. Leo's running point, with Wyatt's and Jaiden's help. Casey and I went to The Ten Mile House to calm down." She kept her tone soft and easy, so as not to spook Ava.

"Heaven's, honey, you didn't drive home intoxicated. Did you?" Her brows furrowed.

"Of course not, Mom; we called a ride. You can drop me by there to pick my car up this morning."

"How did you know I'd be here?"

She bent her head eying her mother over her nose. "Seriously? The way gossip flows in this burg, I wouldn't have been surprised had you showed up during the night. Now, let's get to work. I've got marketing to do on Tray's properties."

♥♥♥♥

Chloe sat working at her computer in her cubical when her phone sounded. "Chloe Roberts here."

"Ms. Roberts, how's your day going?" Tray's deep, soothing New York twang sounded refreshing.

"Fabulous." *If you ignore the dead guy in my future home.* She couldn't get the adorable bungalow out of her mind. "How about yours?" Tray might be the distraction she needed.

Worry filtered his tone. "Are you sure? I heard what you got mixed up in last night. You okay?"

Nodding to herself, she closed her eyes. The grapevine worked its wonders. Every soul in town was aware of Chloe's latest escapade.

Might as well go with the flow.

"So you heard I found a murder victim. I'm glad it wasn't your house." Unlike Chloe, Tray might have walked away. She needed commission from his purchase in order to buy.

"Did you lose your client?" She appreciated angst in his sultry voice. His concern for her welfare felt good. She liked him more each time they talked.

"No, as matter of fact; she's going to write an offer once ownership is established." No need to admit she was the buyer.

"There's the go-getter agent I hired. I knew putting you on my team was smart." He cleared his throat. "How about I take you to dinner? I hear there's a great French Bistro in Sweetwater, and the chef studied in France and traveled the Asian continent cooking in well-known establishments."

"Yes, Mom told me about it. I remember Dovie Fuller. She's a few years older than me. She co-hosted a cooking show in Asia with her ex-husband for a while. I hear the food is excellent at the bistro. What time do you have in mind?" Her heart did a hop-skip-and-jump anticipating an evening with the charming millionaire—or was it billionaire? She should research and find out. Leo might not have time for her, but Tray acted anxious for her company.

"I'll pick you up at seven. Office or home?"

"Home, thanks; I'll text you the address." She would get a shopping fix and a new dress for her date. Was it a date . . . or business? Who cared? Tray was fun and charismatic, the answer to her prayers. A dose of wining and dining was what exactly what she needed.

"Great, see you later. I'm looking forward to it."

She pictured the good-looking, self-assured businessman commanding forces from behind a massive desk. People surrounded him, rushing to do his bidding.

Power was exciting and sexy as all get out.

Casey answered the bell, while Chloe finished her makeup and hair. She tugged her curly mop into a loose chignon in back. Adding a touch of green eyeshadow, she accentuated her dark eyes to coordinate with the clingy,

Kelly-green sheath she bought that afternoon. She wore nude heels, and pearls hung at her neck and ears.

She admired her reflection in the full-length mirror spinning from side to side. The low cut neckline was enticed without being blatantly showy. The color highlighted her tawny skin; and cool, dark silk caressed her curves complimenting her figure.

She had missed feeling attractive and sensual. She'd barely given her appearance a thought during the last year. This was a new life, and she was ready to impress Mr. Ackerson.

Tray propped at the bar sipping a glass of wine Casey had poured. He spun when Chloe entered and extended a bouquet of yellow roses.

Yep definitely a date.

"These are for you." His brilliant smile displayed perfect pearly whites.

"They're lovely. I adore the scent of roses. Thank you." Her heart skipped a note.

A broad smile filled a wide, square jaw engaging tiny smile wrinkles at outer edges of glistening, brown eyes. The sophisticated gentleman was debonair and considerate, and she was touched by his gift.

Hal dressed for the ballet wearing a yellow rose on his lapel, flashed through her mind. Her breath caught. Her chest tightened. For a second she wanted to escape to her room and hide. She sucked in air trying to avoid hyperventilating as she turned toward the counter so Tray wouldn't see her reaction.

Don't embarrass yourself in front of Tray Ackerson. He didn't hire a weak, mental basket case. He mustn't see that side of you. Get it together girl.

She and Hal hadn't officially broken their engagement. Technically they were betrothed, but Hal was gone. After six months, she'd stowed her ring away, figuring she wasn't held to the bargain. Contrary to her mother's and Casey's efforts, she'd resisted dating, not having the slightest interest in men—until Leo and Tray entered her life.

Dead? Missing? Kidnapped? Did he leave me on purpose? By force? She may never know.

She inhaled fragrance allowing it to fill gaps in her that had soured. Living hell over and over again in the last year—and the last twenty-four hours could easily send her spiraling . . . again. This wasn't the time for a panic attack.

Casey kept a conversation going with their guest, probably suspecting what was rambling through Chloe's mind, giving her time to get her shit together. Chloe fumbled through cabinets pretending to search for a vase.

Adorable Deputy, Leo Sanders had sparked her interest, but he'd put her on hold. She understood, but didn't like it. He couldn't take the chance of a conflict of interest and had to prove she wasn't involved in the crime before he could have any kind of association with her. Leo would probably lose interest by the time he cleared the damned thing up, so a relationship with Leo probably wasn't in her future. Tray was here and wanted her attention. The dating pool had definitely improved since she moved away.

Forget the damned future. Stop living in the past. Today is all there is. Live it. Enjoy.

She inhaled. The floral fragrance was like balm to her heart as it attempted to mend itself.

Little things—a sexy, fascinating man; silk against her skin; flowers from a suitor; good food and friends went a long way toward making up for the bad stuff. Compartmentalizing and pushing issues into blocks to deal with as necessary was a technique she'd learned that helped.

Live in the present. Another.

Now—she intended to indulge in a good time.

♥♥♥♥

Tray portrayed an impeccable gentleman escorting Chloe to his Jaguar. His touch on her back sent tiny sparks of giddiness through her system. He held her hand as they strolled into Cabaret de Fuller, and Dovie Fuller showed them to a quiet, candle-lit corner table. Tray held Chloe's chair out.

"This is a lovely restaurant, Ms. Fuller. I've heard the best comments about it." Chloe smiled at the gorgeous redhead handing them menus.

"From what I understand, you're quite the chef. This place smells phenomenal. I can't wait to try your cuisine." Tray shook the petite woman's hand.

"Thank you, please call me Dovie."

"Thank you, Dovie. I'm Tray Ackerson. I'm new in town."

"Welcome, Tray." With a cordial smile Dovie left them to peruse the selection.

When a waitress arrived, they ordered coq au vin appetizers, grilled steaks with garlic-chive butter and French potato salad. For dessert they chose buttery madeleines with vanilla crème brulée and a bottle of red wine.

As they talked before the food came, he held her hand on the tabletop. Warmth from his large paw seeped into Chloe. She was in the right place at the right time.

Tray carefully avoided reference to her previous evening and all mention of business. They discussed movies, plays, music and sports. Their shared interest in all things connected to water sports was a good sign. Tray enjoyed horseback riding and skeet shooting as much as Chloe did.

"When it gets warmer we'll take in a couple days on my houseboat on Cumberland Lake. It's a fine place for water skiing."

"That sounds amazing. You have a houseboat and a ski boat?" Chloe mentally calculated what it must cost to purchase and moor his elaborate toys. It was more than she'd made in the last couple years total.

"Yes, I dock the ski boat beside the houseboat." He acted nonchalant, as though it was no big deal.

"I haven't skied in years. I hear it's like riding a bike." Her heart did a happy dance at him including her in future plans and a tingle sped down her spine.

"Do you know Justin Henderson?" He asked over their meal.

"Sure, I remember him from when I was a kid. I saw him at his bar last night. Why?"

"Poor guy, I heard he lost a leg in a motorcycle accident." Tray acted properly saddened.

"Yes, tragic. A speeding station wagon pulled in front of him. Justin's lucky he's here. The first officer on scene believed he was dead. He's got a great prosthetic though. He was dancing up a storm with his wife, Corrie last night." It had warmed her heart seeing the couple so much in love. They'd been through their own individual hells and come out the other side to find a new life—and love. Would she fare as well?

"Justin doesn't let it stop him. I'm living out of a hotel and temporarily joined a town gym. Justin is there every morning like clockwork, lifting weights, walking on the treadmill and doing all sorts of things." Tray shook his head looking impressed.

"Disability doesn't stop him from doing what he wants. Mom said he still rides horses. He removes the leg and stores it in a holster attached to the saddle."

"You're right. I've ridden with him. In fact, Justin is boarding my stallion until I move. We rode around his property last week. Then we galloped down the road and across Mane Lane Farm, where we ate lunch with his wife, Corrie; her brother, Levi; and Levi's wife, Riley."

"Isn't it a beautiful farm?" She had yet to meet the mysterious Riley, who had snagged long-time bachelor, Levi Madison.

A wistful sigh filtered from her reminiscing about Mane Lane Farm's massive rolling pastures of Kentucky bluegrass surrounded by expansive rows of white board fencing. She could almost smell fresh cut grass and magnolia blossoms from trees sporadically positioned throughout fields. Magnificent steeds grazed unaware of the splendor of their surroundings. One occasionally glimpsed a finely painted, manicured, majestic barn, looking more elaborate and costly than most homes she'd seen.

"It's spectacular, and they have impressive, high-tech security."

"They need it, doing a multi-billion-dollar business breeding racing livestock. They breed for owners from around the world and own several champion top studs, quite a few successful racers, and a herd of personal race and show horses. The sperm bank alone profits in the billions per year—a fascinating industry."

He nodded with a pleasant smile. "I see you're up on racing and equestrian stats. A smart woman knows the size of the prize. Levi Madison gave me the name of his security firm. I'm planning to have them set up a system at my new home." It didn't surprise her, and was like Levi to be generous.

"Hey, a gal can't grow up in the horse capital of the world and not understand the trade. I listen, learn and have a curious mind about things spurring my interest."

Tray didn't seem the insecure type. Levi Madison was the only other millionaire she knew personally. She'd sold properties to wealthy and celebrity clients in New York, but knowledge of requirements of the rich only extended to her ability to find suitable properties based on criteria they'd provided. This wasn't a high-crime area, but who was she to argue need for professional security? She'd found a dead guy last night.

"Have you considered having a horse of your own?" His thumb enticingly caressed the top of her hand resting on the table.

Little tingles of delight danced up her arm. It was good being the object of a man's attention again. It had been too long.

"I'd love it, but upkeep is expensive. I don't have a place to board one."

"If you change your mind, I'm bringing mine home when I move in. He'd love a buddy to stay with him. I hate not providing him company and would happily board yours so Zen would have a pal to keep him happy."

It would be convenient, if she and Tray turned out to be good for each other, but it was too soon to commit. She was barely getting her dating feet wet again.

"Wow, that's generous of you? I'll think on it. I can't afford one now. First, I've got to get a home of my own. I'm staying with Casey until I purchase something."

He blinked as though not having considered expense of ownership. Of course, he wouldn't. Money was of little concern to Tray Ackerson. His smile returned. "Anything speak to you yet?"

Glancing away she visualized the cottage with its retro tile; light, airy space; large back yard and amazing kitchen. She grinned and nodded. "As a matter of fact, there's a house I'm considering. I'll let you know how it shakes out."

After dinner, again holding her hand he escorted her to his fancy ride. Heat swarmed up her arm and straight to her heart. A bit of it mellowed in her tummy. Some was the wine they'd shared. Mostly it was the dynamic man beside her. She relaxed and felt unusually at ease with her new friend.

At Casey's condo he escorted her to the entrance. She pulled her key out. Taking it, he inserted it in the lock. Pushing the door barely ajar, he returned the key, and his hand cupped hers. The other grazed her shoulders, and a finger slid across her collar bone.

A tingle shot straight to her core forcing a sudden inhale.

He trailed sensitive skin along her chin. Tilting her head bending he grazed lips barely across hers. "Ummm," he moaned with lips still touching.

Contact transformed into a soft caress of mouths. Moving closer, enveloping her with his arms, he lifted her slightly off the ground and pressed her close to his body. The kiss deepened with a slip of his tongue sliding gently across and delving momentarily inside. With a quick peck, he placed her back on her feet.

She enjoyed kissing and being treated preciously. She inhaled, and her eyes closed briefly. As she returned to the real world, angst settled in.

Take it slow.

He winked and released her. Did he her mind?

Heaven forbid.

She was again able to breathe and realized she'd been holding air. Her brows rose and fell, and with a hearty intake, her shoulders rocked back. "Goodnight, Tray."

He was already high-stepping gaily along the walk. "Goodnight, Chloe. We'll talk tomorrow." The guy had confidence and knew how to leave a gal hankering for more.

She entered and closed the door behind her. Glancing out the side window, his tail lights became visible. Her butt leaned against the wall, and her eyes closed. A couple deep lungs full of air restored her equilibrium. She smiled as she mulled over the flawless evening with her gallant suitor.

Tray wasn't Hal—nothing like him, except maybe his confidant air. Hal wasn't perfect. She had to let him go.

Attraction to the charming entrepreneur sent tingles to her toes. High time something happened right for her.

CHAPTER 10

Chloe leaned on the counter sipping her first cup of Joe. Casey grabbed her things to run out the door. She stalled when her phone rang.

"Hi, Casey here. Sure, I've got time before my first patient. I'll stop on the way to the hospital. Yeah, she's here. Want to talk with her? Okay. See ya in a few." She clicked off nodding toward it. Chloe's phone rang. "It's Leo. He asked me to come in for questioning. He said he was going to call you. Hey, I want to hear all about your date with your client. Unfortunately I have to run. Later, Gator, I'm off. Enjoy." Casey flipped the door wide and was gone.

Reference to Tray brought a cringe out of Chloe. She'd broken one of her main rules with him, never to date someone she had a professional relationship with; but she'd seriously needed wining and dining yesterday. Resisting would've been pointless. Tray was used to getting his way. He wouldn't have stopped with a no from her.

Chloe clicked the phone on and stood erect eager. Leo's adorable Kentucky accent no matter the situation had a soothing effect on her. She hadn't totally tossed aside the idea of dating him—yet.

"Howdy, Deputy Sanders, Casey said you wanted me to call. What can I do for you?" She chirped happily relaxing against the sofa.

"Hey, Chloe, sorry to keep it strictly business, but I have questions for you concerning my case. Could you stop by the station this morning?" His stiff, businesslike tone was not what she'd hoped for.

"Sure. I'll be around lunchtime."

What should she wear? She had potential clients to impress and was surprised how excited she was anticipating her meeting with Leo. She would drop by the station around eleven-thirty before folks broke for lunch, maybe she could snag one-on-one time with him. If he played his cards right, she'd let him buy her a meal.

Beige pumps and a burgundy sheath showing off her curves, Chloe entered the police station like a derby winner after a big race. She neared the front desk. A uniformed Jaiden Coldwater entered behind her.

"Hey, gal, you here to see Sanders?" She wore a brilliant smile.

"Yes, Leo asked me to come in."

The petite, half-Choctaw, weapon-clad woman's soft, slow speech made her approachable and likable, even with the powerful aura she exuded. It was easy recognizing how residents were comfortable relying on her.

"Awesome, follow me. I'll show you to his cubical." The deputy pushed the door to the bullpen open.

Military-style, metal desks filled a room lined with file cabinets and a large printer. Sheriff Gordon chatted on a phone behind his desk in a glass-walled office at the far end. Several deputies worked at stations.

Leo's was easily spotted at a cube near Wyatt's. As the door open, he glanced up, waved and grinned.

"Hey, Jaiden; how's it going? Ms. Roberts, come over." He motioned to a chair inside his space. "Have a seat."

Ms. Roberts? Whose benefit was that for?

"See you later." Jaiden patted Chloe's arm as she started toward Sanders. Jaiden walked to hers and plopped into a chair.

"Good morning, Leo. What happened to calling me Chloe?" She shook his hand then took the chair he indicated disappointed his touch didn't thrill her like it previously had.

"Sorry, this is business. Let's keep it professional. Thanks for coming in." He winked casually as though he'd forgotten. His tone was a bit less formal. "This won't take long. I need to clear up a few things. We'll have you out of here in no time."

"Great. Almost lunchtime anyway, I'm due a break."

Too pushy?

He ignored the hint and smiled, sorting through a stack of files. Pulling one out, he flipped through it and made a series of inquiries, taking notes as she answered.

Did he need hitting over the head? She'd cued him to invite her. Maybe he had other plans.

"Let's see. You said you didn't recognize the victim."

"That's right. I understand you've identified him."

"Yes, Harvey Carnes was the owner and was in the process of divorcing his wife, Helen. Do you know or recognize either of them or their names?" He studied her like trying to read her with a natural, casual air, so at ease and to the point it had to be an interrogation technique.

The method worked the opposite with her. She stiffened in her seat. "No, I don't know them. I recognize the name *Carnes* listed on the MLS sheet as 'Owner Name.'"

"I see. What about the name Sandy Bennet?"

"I don't know her and the name wasn't familiar until that night. If I'm not mistaken, I saw her at The Ten Mile House after we left the scene. She was sloppy drunk and ranting about Harvey's wife killing him and trashing her car. I couldn't help overhearing. Everyone did. I figured her for the victim's girlfriend from the accusation."

His brow arched. "You went drinking after leaving the murder scene?"

She shrugged casually as his attitude allowed. "Yes, Casey and I felt like a drink, and we couldn't face the quiet at home. We needed to be around people."

He nodded soberly. "I see. Mr. Carnes worked for the Foundation Corporation. Do you know anyone connected to the company? Corporate headquarters is in Lexington, and there's a branch in New York City. Mr. Carnes was employed in Lexington."

"I can't recall. It sounds familiar. It might be one of the vendors Mr. Ackerson contracts. I'm not sure. You'll need to ask Tray. I'm sorry. I'm not familiar with anyone else connected to the business."

"Tray?" Disapproval painted his delightful emerald eyes with something she hoped was jealousy. He bounced the end of an ink pen against pursed lips. His head tilted then straightened. Eyes narrowed lost in deep thought. "Please tell me about Mr. Ackerson."

The way he eyed her spurred optimism this was more than a professional discussion. A connection flickered between them. His personal, intimate tone showed worry for her safety—more than police business. It filled the air, and controlled his expression.

She wanted to touch the hand of the kind, laid-back man, finding him surprisingly attractive under the circumstances. He was obviously torn between duty and personal emotion. She longed to run a finger across his adorable laugh lines and spend time together chatting about what they had in common—anything but the reason she was there. They could be more than acquaintances, given the chance.

"Yes, I recently sold him a house. He's relocating from New York City and developing a sizable subdivision of single-family homes, townhouses and condos. I've listed the real estate as his selling agent. We recently reviewed his processes and financials. Unless I'm mistaken, Tray uses services of the Foundation Corporation. That's my sole reference." Biting the side of her mouth, she racked her brain for helpful information; but it was all she recollected.

"You have a professional relationship with Tray Ackerson?" She didn't like his stern look, preferring the previous casual approach.

And personal.

"Yes." All Deputy Sanders needed to know.

"How long have you known him?" His head cricked sideways, and his words sounded measured.

"Only a short while; here's Mr. Ackerson's business card." She pulled one from a side pocket of her purse and handed it to Leo. It slipped from her grasp floating toward the floor. She bent to retrieve it.

Leo jerked forward toward the card. Their heads clashed.

She blinked jolting backward. The room went black for an instant. Then she blinked stars away. Her fuzzy swooned, and air gushed from her.

"Ouch." Her hand snapped to cover her noggin where it had made contact. She blinked several times clearing her vision.

Leo's comforting hands on her arms steadied her. His mouth widened like those gorgeous eyes that mesmerized her like hypnosis one feels staring at flames of a bonfire.

His warm paws lingered on her forearms, as he helped her into her seat.

Heat welled deep in her belly, wishing he'd pull her into his arms to hold her tight—just for a moment; but he didn't. She expelled a hearty gush of air.

"Chloe, I'm sorry. I'm a klutz. Please forgive me. You okay?" He rubbed the side of his crown with a hand. The other rested against her bare shoulder sending warmth oozing to her chest like glowing embers from a backyard campfire and easing her pain. He'd called her by her first name.

Shaking remaining stun from her head, she smiled amiably. Something genuine from his soul radiated through the greenest eyes she'd ever seen, assuring Chloe she could trust the man where others had failed her.

Hal's face and Dad's flashed through her mind. She shook the images off. Surely all men wouldn't disappoint.

"I'm fine. No worries. Where were we? Oh, yeah, reach out to Tray. He might help with the company you mentioned. I don't know anything more."

Leo hesitated letting go and easing into his chair.

With is release, air-conditioning quickly cooled her flesh, instantly missing Leo's blaze. Inhaling, she sat erect, recalling where they were. She glanced about catching the other officers in the bullpen turning back to their work. The show was over.

Leo slid the card into his lap drawer. "Will do. Thanks. You toured the Carnes house for yourself. Right?"

"Right."

"You never met Mr. or Mrs. Carnes previously. Correct?"

"Correct."

"I don't suppose you have interest in the property any longer." He studied her face.

"That's incorrect. A death doesn't physical damage it. Some might have concerns; but the roof won't leak because of what happened there. The property is in the same shape. It doesn't bother me Mr. Cares died there. He's at the morgue, and I'm sure a cleanup crew will manage the rest. I like the residence, the neighborhood is located conveniently for my needs, and it's within my budget. I'm evaluating pros and cons and considering making an offer but hesitate to approach Mrs. Carnes in her time of grief."

Steepling fingers, putting elbows on his desktop, he rested his chin on them and deliberated for a few seconds. A devilish grin lit his face. That smile must've stopped many a female heart before hers. Her belly did a happy dance, and her heartbeat skipped a note.

"You surprise me. I knew you for a smart businesswoman. It's unusual for a young female being willing to live in a murder house. Lots of folks would be wary."

She laughed easily. "Unless a serial killer is targeting occupants of that particular house, I see no reason to fear it. Mr. Carnes is unlikely to haunt me. If he did, what harm could he do?"

"*I ain't afraid a no ghost.*" He chuckled. "We're not figuring this for a serial kill." His hearty laughter mocking the hilarious Ghostbusters movie made her long to linger in his company and find other ways to make him smile. At least he acted impressed. It was a good thing.

Cute as a newborn colt, Leo Sanders' long, lanky limbs were nearly as graceful. She imagined him sauntering along a country lane toting a fishing-pole in one hand and tackle box in another—and maybe her walking beside him.

"Good to know; is there a problem with purchasing the property, assuming the ex is willing?"

With raised brows he shook his head. "Absolutely not; the coroner's report defined the time of death. We need to rule you out as a suspect. Where were you on Wednesday afternoon?"

"In Lexington taking my real estate exam—it's easy enough to verify."

"I'll get on it, so we can mark you off the long list. I've spoken with the grieving widow a couple times since we found Harvey. She's not emotionally distraught and would probably be thrilled to hear your offer. I wouldn't put it off. Since Harvey is deceased and on the deed with her, she might need to wait until probate authorizes her right to sell before accepting."

"Terrific. I'll submit my offer to her agent." So there were several suspects; thank goodness she'd be cleared soon.

As if on cue, a woman burst into the bullpen trailed by a uniformed deputy. She glanced around. Noticing Leo had a visitor, she shrugged and stomped toward Wyatt's office. Seeing her approach, he stood at his desk. She didn't bother knocking, but whipped the door open.

"Speak of the devil." Leo's words were whispered.

Wyatt spoke to the policeman on her tail. "It is okay, Bob. I'll take care of our lovely guest." He paid attention to his obviously unexpected guest. "Mrs. Carnes, good to see you. Please come in. What can I do for you?" She slammed the door, and vibrations were felt all the way to Leo's desk.

Glass walls did little to deafen shouting. "That cunt, Sandy Bennet keyed my car and busted my light. I want her arrested. The floozy killed my husband."

Wyatt coaxed the distraught widow into a chair and managed to quiet her. His swarthy appearance and charming demeanor worked miracles, especially with women.

Leo shrugged, and his face glowed red.

Chloe snickered. "You dodged a bullet. She was heading for you. Lucky Wyatt." She shook her hand in the air.

Leo's head bobbed. He glanced toward Wyatt' office then back at Chloe. "Better the sheriff than me. He can handle her. Wyatt could calm a cobra with a few sweet words. That's your grieving widow, Helen Carnes, wife of your murder victim."

"Wow, she's in a state alright—and not because of her husband's demise. He's dead, and she's still pissed about his cheating."

"She believes Sandy Bennet did the deed. Apparently the two gals had a cat fight. Sandy says Harvey told her he was getting divorced to marry her. Discovering the dude wasn't separated from his wife, Sandy confronted him and Helen together. The gals went at it. Harvey broke them apart, but repercussions occurred."

He wasn't tell her anything she couldn't learn from the gossip mill. Thank goodness she didn't have to negotiate in person with the hostile female.

"Does Helen think Harvey deserved what he got? By repercussions do you mean Sandy keying Helen's car and busting her lights?"

"Apparently, but we have no proof. They've accused each other. Sandy swears Helen did Harvey in previously accused Helen of puncturing her tires. Again, we have no proof of the automobile incident. Neither of them has an alibi for when Harvey was murdered."

"I heard that at the tavern. A drunken female spouted off about it at The Ten Mile House. I imagined she was Harvey's lover—Sandy. I wasn't sure at the time. Did one of them shoot him?"

"We're checking all angles."

"I suppose so. Isn't the spouse usually the prime suspect? In a crime of passion wouldn't she unload the gun into him? I noticed one bullet hole, when I found the body. Of course, I didn't inspect the corpse thoroughly."

"Good observation. You watch a lot of NCIS? Do ya?" He chuckled. The adorable Opie smile engaged dimples she would enjoy seeing more of.

"I like an enticing mystery now and again but prefer it not be real life."

"Speaking of which, what did your mom say about you buying a murder house?" He didn't bother holding back a snicker.

"She's probably going to freak. I haven't told her yet, but I can handle it. No worries. I'd appreciate you keeping it between us. I'd like to break it to Mom on my own terms, only if my offer is accepted."

"Your secret is safe. Good luck. I hope you get the house, if you sincerely want it." He crossed his heart with a finger and stood signaling the interview was over. She was free to go. He wasn't about to ask her to lunch—apparently.

She accepted his earnest handshake. His skin was warm and dry; his movement confident. He held on an instant longer than necessary. Maybe he hated letting her go, much as she hated leaving.

She wanted to know Leo better. This wasn't the time or place for engaging relationships. He was the officer in charge of a murder investigation she was tied to, whether she liked it or not. Still, she was intrigued; but being a suspect, she couldn't wrangle lunch or any other kind of date out of him.

It was for the best. A wave of sadness swam through her brain. Where did she get off flirting with the amusing deputy?

Hal was . . . where the hell was Hal anyway? Would she ever get him out of her system? She'd done the work to find closure. He needed to release his bond from her. She sighed heavily forcing Hal from her mind.

Leo returned attention to his computer, leaving her to go. Chloe glanced around. Jaiden was typing at her desk, so Chloe sauntered over.

"Hey, gal, you eat yet? Want to grab something quick?"

Jaiden smiled, making Chloe wish she had thick lips and skin not needing a tan. The mass of dark curls forced into a thick bun at the nape of Jaiden's head looked like it wanted to spring wildly loose around her beautiful face.

"Actually I'm starved. The guys ate, so I'm on my own for lunch. How about the Royal Diner across the street?" Jaiden locked her laptop in a drawer and picked her phone up.

"Perfect. Is it okay with me being on the suspect list?"

"Casey said you took your test Wednesday. I pulled the state's records a few minutes ago, confirming you spent the afternoon in the testing room. We're good." With a hand on Chloe's arm she signaled her toward the exit.

Relief washed over Chloe, though she couldn't imagine why. She had done no wrong.

"Great. Can you share that tidbit with Deputy Sanders, please?"

Jaiden snickered and saluted. "Will do. Did he give you a hard time?"

Chloe shrugged. "Maybe a little."

Jaiden would mark her off the list and share the information with Wyatt and Leo. Maybe Leo would grow more susceptible to her charms—assuming he had time to think while heading up the search for a killer in their midst. She hoped so—on both accounts.

The women strolled the short distance to Sadie's diner and selected a window booth overlooking the street. After saying hello to friends and giving Sadie their orders, they relaxed deeper into cozy benches. Spring rays gleamed through the plate-glass window warming them.

"I adore this time of year. Everything is fresh and new. Life sprouts from everywhere. Babies are born of almost every species, and grass smells delightful while it paints valleys green. I can't wait for May. I'll plant flowers around the house and watch them bloom all summer." Jaiden sighed.

"I hope I have a house to plant flowers around by May. I'm going to make an offer on one. If it doesn't take too long to close, I should move in by Mother's Day." She envisioned a backyard cookout to celebrate with the yard filled with friends—Casey; Jaiden and her fella, Clay; Mom; Wyatt and his wife, Sage; agents from her office and their mates; maybe Tray and Leo. Would either of them be in her life when the time rolled around?

Jaiden's dark eyes lit up. "Fabulous news; I'm glad you're planting roots. It's a delightful community. I'm happy I came."

"Mom tells me your brother and mother moved here, too. I understand he works for Levi Madison at Mane Lane Farm."

"Yep, Cal is responsible for training Levi's derby champion a couple years ago. They've had several big winners and almost won a triple-crown since Cal took over. Levi is a master breeder, sought out worldwide for his skill; but Cal's expertise is teaching contenders."

"Cal sounds extremely talented."

"That he is. I'm proud of my big brother." She flipped her phone out showing a photo.

The dark, handsome, Native American man's strapping frame was clad in a denim shirt and jeans. Black tresses hanging across broad shoulders to his waist caught light. A muscular arm snuggled a petite woman with biased-cut hair the same shade as his with a portion streaked with purple along one side of her face. Wearing funky, gothic clothing and a dog collar around her neck, she gazed lovingly at her towering husband.

"This is Cal and Rose. Rose works for Wyatt's wife, Sage at Parsley, Sage, Rose, Mary & Wine. The farm produces organic grapes for local winemakers and harvests and sells herbs, spices and vegetables. They make farmer's cheese and goat cheese."

"I hear Sage is a booming success."

"Yes, she's a dynamo. She moved here with a master's degree in agri-something and several years' experience working for the FDA in an agricultural role. She has contacts and knows how to make things happen."

"Mom says Sage lands in the middle of trouble when it hits."

"Yes, Wyatt is probably counting his blessings Sage isn't involved in this current murder. He's protective of her, but calls her a danger magnet." Obviously Jaiden respected and liked her boss and his wife.

"I can't wait until this thing is over. How long does it take to solve a murder? It's giving me the creeps." Chloe shivered.

"I know what you mean. I'm anxious, but one can't press these things. It takes a good amount of time putting facts together, building a clean case to put the correct person away. Every detail must be handled perfect, by the book and flawless. No telling how long it will take."

So much for her notion of dating Leo, she might as well forget it; and the killer was still on the loose.

They ate and discussed fun things to do in Sweetwater and planned another outing with Casey for the following week.

The brilliant diamond on Jaiden's left hand caught the sun's rays and sparkled. "Tell me about your man." Chloe nodded its direction.

"Ah, Doc . . . he's such a sweetheart. Clay Barnes is a surgeon the same age as Wyatt, Levi and Justin Henderson, and grew up here with them. He's tall, thin with short, blond hair, and he's quiet, sweet and considerate to a fault—kind of nerdy in an appealing way. He sets me on fire like no stud I ever met. After surgical residency in Chicago, he returned home to settle his parents' estate and discovered he enjoyed working in a small town. We got together and fell smack-dab, face-first in love. I can't imagine life without Clay." Gushing, her eyes glistened, and her already high cheekbones plumped.

"When's the big date?"

Jaiden laughed and exhaled. "You know what? Clay and I stay so damned busy. It's all we can do to wear each other out in bed. We haven't gotten around to setting a date. The year has flown by. About time we talk timing. I'll get the ball rolling this weekend, if I get free time with the investigation going on."

"Let me know if there's anything I can do. I adore weddings." Chloe was excited for her new friend.

Oh, to be in love.

Jaiden laid a hand across Chloe's. "Thank you. That's sweet. I appreciate it. I'll keep it in mind."

"Now, tell me about Leo Sanders. The boy is Grade A, All American Prime. Is he attached?"

Please say no.

Casey had told her he was single, but she could be wrong. Chloe was getting mixed signals from the man. She needed to know before wasting time on him.

Chuckling, Jaiden glanced at the station. On cue, Leo trotted down the few steps to the street.

A poodle puppy dragging a leash behind it sped around the corner heading into traffic. Leo's long legs stretched, racing for the animal. A vehicle rounded the corner. Leo bent and snatched the tiny dog into his arms then threw himself out of harm's way toward the curb. Quick thinking and lightning reflexes saved the puppy's life—and risked Leo's. From its angle with cars blocking view, the driver never would've seen the tiny creature in time to avoid hitting it.

A little girl followed by a woman raced around the corner toward him. The girl was crying as she took the feisty animal and snuggled it tight against her chubby cheeks. The lady acted flustered as she hugged Leo and thanked the officer for saving their pet. The unconcerned puppy joyously lapped kisses across the girl's chirrup face. Leo nodded, nonchalantly then climbed into his cruiser and sped away like it was nothing.

Mesmerized as the scene played out, Chloe's mouth fell open. Her eyes widened. The man is a freaking hero. "Leo sure has moves—quick and light on his feet, and graceful too."

Jaiden chuckled. "Leo to the rescue—I wondered how long it would take you to check him out. There he goes, playing hero in front of your eyes. I figured you were going sweet on our Deputy Sanders at the bowling alley."

Chloe shrugged, noncommittally, sure Jaiden heard her pounding heartbeat. "A girl has to weigh her options."

"I don't blame you one bit. Leo's a super guy. He's a hard worker, pleasant as can be, and level headed—all in all an honorable man."

"Is he seeing anyone?" There was the ten-million-dollar question.

"He went out occasionally with some chick who works at the theater. They broke up ages ago. Not a big deal. He hasn't dated lately or gotten serious about anyone . . . for years. I'd say the field is wide open. Get your rope out and lasso that boy, Chloe." She laughed pretending to swirl an invisible rope with her hand.

Chloe chuckled at the image. "I'll work on it. This town has decent options." Her attention diverted by the door clanging shut.

A familiar male strutted into the diner acting like he owned the place. Tall, thin and a bit too tan, Carl Townsend tilted his cowboy hat at Sadie and stopped by a couple tables speaking with customers. Spotting Chloe and Jaiden, he ambled to their booth.

"I'll be damned, Chloe Roberts, I heard tell you'd come home to roost. I'll be dog-gone if you ain't a sight for sore eyes." His thumbs tucked into a western belt, and he rocked backward on heels of worn boots. He whipped his hat off and placed it on the end of the table upside down. Without invitation, his lanky body slid in beside Chloe. An arm circled her back across the top of the seat.

A shiver zipped down her spine. Their thighs met. A spark flew from his leg into hers on contact. She jerked her leg away and scrambled closer to the window to accommodate him. Chloe felt like she'd swallowed her burger whole and might choke on the wad. She inhaled through her nose trying to gain control.

"Hello, Carl; do you know Jaiden?"

Jaiden acted dubious tilting her head forward and eying them from below her eyelids. "Mr. Townsend." She nodded Carl's way. From her expression, she'd put two-and-two together.

Chloe glanced around knowing customers watched. They didn't appear to be, but the Sweetwater gossip mill was brewing with silence in the vast dining room. Sadie shook her head and rolled her eyes before disappearing into the kitchen.

Carl was too chummy for her taste. They were nothing to each other. How she had ever considered him date-worthy? He was nowhere near her type.

"Of course, everyone knows Deputy Coldwater. She's famous and quite the heroine more than once since moving to Sweetwater. How you doing, Jaiden?" He made it sound like they were old pals.

"I'm well, Carl. How's the family?" Jaiden faced him without expression, clearly not a fan either.

He stared at the table. "The young 'uns are getting over a spring cold. Stacy is good, good old Stacy." He gave attention to Chloe with an expression she hoped to be hunger but feared was longing to renew an old relationship. "How the hell are you, Chloe? I'm sorry to hear you lost your man in New York. I'm thrilled you're home, though. It's where you belong, honey child." His arm snaked around her shoulders and the hand fingered her bare skin, making her wish she hadn't worn a sleeveless dress.

She pulled herself free methodically without speaking, holding back a shiver. Looking him square in the eye. "Thanks, I'm happy being here." She glanced at Jaiden who stifled a snicker. They should have chosen a table instead of a booth. "I bumped into Stacy, but we didn't have much opportunity to chat. How many children do you and she have?" Dumb ass shouldn't need constant reminder he was a family man.

"Yeah, I heard she ran into you at The Ten Mile House. I can imagine how it went. She had way too much to drink. Boy, was she in a mood when she made it home? I hope she didn't do nothing rash." He squished his lips together.

"We had words." Chloe nodded. "It wasn't pleasant."

"If she offended you, I'm sorry. You know how Stacy is—especially about you. Anyway, I heard about the dead dude. I'm concerned about you. You could be in danger. I hear tell the SOB had plenty of enemies, but it could be a random thing or a serial murder." His hand slid down grazing her thigh.

She flinched. He tried snuggling against her. Wiggling her shoulders she squeezed her purse between them.

She wasn't having this. Flirting had to stop.

He released his hand, allowing his arm to continue resting along the back of the bench, causing hair on the back of her neck to stand on edge.

111

"Thanks; there's nothing to worry about. I found the body, but I'm not connected to the actual murder. Nor am I in danger. I had nothing to do with it and didn't know the character. I'm fine, and police will arrest whoever did it soon." Her eyes begged Jaiden to rescue her.

"We're scrutinizing viable suspects and exploring angles. We believe Chloe is in no danger. Of course, until we determine who did this, the town should stay wary. You might want to address it with your wife. She should watch her surroundings, especially if she's out on the town, like the other evening. We don't need additional victims turning up. Speaking of the case, Chloe and I have appointments. Excuse us, please." She snatched the bill Sadie had dropped off from under her plate and reached for Chloe's. "My treat." She winked toward Chloe as she stood.

Carl had no recourse but to move and allow Chloe to leave. She followed Jaiden, and Carl returned to his seat waiting for Sadie to take his order. His big, brown, cow eyes made Chloe exhale a sigh.

"Give Stacy my best, Carl." She spoke loud enough for diners to hear from the doorway, then exited without giving him time to respond. Jaiden was hot on her heels.

"Was that stooge hitting on you?" Jaiden's mouth and eyes snapped wide.

"He could've simply been alarmed, but it felt like he was coming on to me. He's married. It gives me the creeps. I get a sleazy feeling from Carl. We dated in school, but there was nothing serious between us. We've changed, and I'm having trouble recalling what I saw in him. Yuk." She shivered at the icicle slithering down her spine.

"His wife is the broad who ripped you a new one at The Ten Mile House. Right?" She was holding back laughter, but it appeared difficult.

"Yep. He's an old flame that ended when I left for university. What we had was a teen romance at best."

"His wife doesn't see it that way. You sure he's gotten over you?" Jaiden's evil grin proved she was teasing and getting a kick out of the incident.

"I'm glad you're having fun. He got too intimate for a married guy. He's off limits, and I've no interest anyway. Besides, his wife hates me—always has, though I'm not sure why. Can't say he has good taste. Stacy Smyth was a bitch, a bully and a snob; but she was popular. Her family is wealthy with old, racing money."

"So you don't have a thing for this Carl?" Jaiden made googly eyes at her.

Chloe slapped her sleeve playfully. "Honey, I've had a hell of a year. My finance disappeared without a trace. I'm starting to be attracted to men again, but definitely not Carl. Stacy's welcome to him. I hope they're happy together. I don't want any part of her or her husband." Chloe shook her head in emphasis.

"Good for you. This sweet town has much better fish to fry." Jaiden was right about that. Between Deputy Leo Sanders and Tray Ackerson, Chloe had viable prospects and was keeping her options open.

After a good laugh, they hugged then returned to their perspective jobs.

Chloe made a mental note to discuss Carl with Casey and her mother. If there was a problem in the Townsend household, they would've heard gossip going around. She didn't want trouble with Carl or Stacy. Carl needed to point that busy-body-nose of his in any direction but hers. Hopefully Carl and Stacy were happily enjoying marital bliss, staying busy cleaning snotty noses—out of Chloe's hair.

"How's it going?" Wyatt folded his hands on his desk.

Leo relaxed in his guest chair. "Folks were more than willing to share scandalous tidbits. I've heard the latest. The new real estate agent finding a corpse was a hot topic. Most everyone questioned shared opinions on who was guilty. Not many facts pertaining to the incident, however." He picked up his notes from his lap and stood.

"It's our job to glean the useful from juice being spread and disregard the rest."

"Got it, boss." He walked back to his desk.

One iota of chatter he could not disregard for personal reasons—Chloe was reported in the company of a dashing fella driving an extravagant sports car. Leo's stomach soured when he heard.

He liked Chloe and had hopes of spending time getting to know the spunky, petite minx. He wasn't sure he could compete with a wealthy bachelor with no baggage and a lavish life to offer. Why did it have to be Tray Ackerson?

Leo came with baggage, and lots of responsibilities as well. Would a gal like Chloe Roberts be interested in a guy with so many ties binding him? If he didn't solve this case soon, it might be too late to try. What little impression he'd been able to make on her would've long faded, and she'd be securely tied to another man. A chill ran through him.

He chuckled at hearing of a shouting match between Chloe and the Townsend woman. Leo didn't think much of Stacy, who flaunted her sexuality. She drank too much; but as far as he knew, never cheated on Carl. Leo dreaded the inevitable, when he'd catch her intoxicated behind the wheel.

He couldn't figure the trio out. What trouble was brewing between Stay, Carl and Chloe? They didn't run in the same crowd.

It surprised him someone mentioned Chloe cozying up with Carl Townsend at Sadie's diner. Surely they got it wrong. Chloe didn't seem the type to go after a married man. Leo couldn't visualize her with Carl—an odd couple for sure. If it was true, no wonder Stacy lit into Chloe at the tavern.

He should ask Jaiden. He wouldn't pry—only enough to get a handle on the strange bits and pieces of chin wagging going around. Jaiden was Chloe's friend. She'd want to clear the air if things were misconstrued.

Leo's fingers itched to ring Chloe up and ask her out. His hand curled and rested on his belly, as his center heated at the notion of spending time with Chloe Richards. Her soft, sensual mouth came to mind—the color of Caribbean coral. He bit his lower lip and closed his eyes. She was worth the effort. He hadn't been this giddy about a female since meeting Claire.

The damned case was crimping his style.

.

CHAPTER 11

"Thanks for picking me up, Mom. How's Gran doing?"

Ava patted her daughter's thigh and pulled into her mother's parking space. "Mom's the same. How are you? How did it go with Deputy Sanders?"

Chloe's face had a mind of its own and went into a genuine smile. Her attraction to Leo Sanders was surprising, especially since he hadn't sought her out. She couldn't shake the feeling he was interested in her and was doing a damned good job hiding it. She'd lay odds on it.

"It was fine. He asked about my relationship with Mr. and Mrs. Carnes. I explained I didn't know them." They retrieved their contribution to dinner from the back seat and moved toward Gran's door carrying rolls and salad.

"I thought you and Leo were hitting it off. How's that going?"

"I thought so too. I've been cleared of suspicion; but he's busy working the case and doesn't have time for me. Maybe he's not as into me as I thought." She grimaced.

"Too bad, dear; maybe the situation will change soon." She put a hand on Chloe's shoulder, and Chloe smiled at her mother.

No need to encourage interference. Ava got in the middle of Chloe's affairs enough already. If only Leo would find the killer, maybe she'd have a chance with him. A lengthy case would give him time to forget why he was interested in the first place.

"Welcome, girls. I'm happy to see you." Angelica answered her door, smartly dressed, perfectly coiffed and made up. Chloe hoped she'd have as flawless skin at her grandmother's age.

They did a round of cheek kisses. Chloe and Ava placed their dishes on the table. Angelica poured goblets from the bar and handed red wine to her guests.

"Thanks, Mom. Chloe, did Leo want anything else?" Ava eyed her suspiciously.

"He asked about a company called Foundation Corporation."

Angelica's eyes blinked. "That's Tony's company." She nonchalantly sipped her wine and took a seat in her favorite chair. Her slim ankles crossed and her legs leaned to the side.

Ava ogled her mother with disbelief and concern, ignoring her comment. Turning to Chloe, she gave a sideways glance at the ceiling. Her mouth crimped.

Poor Gran was getting more confused by the day. Ava moved the conversation forward, "It sounds familiar. Aren't they out of Lexington?"

Chloe shrugged. "Yes. Mr. Carnes worked there. Tray Ackerson sources work to the firm on his projects."

"Oh, so Leo will want to talk with Tray."

"Yes, I gave him Tray's business card. He'll follow up." Turning to Angelica, Chloe sniffed the air. "Gran, the food smells delicious. Is it lasagna?" Her mouth watered at garlic and pasta sauce scent.

"Absolutely, darling." Angelica stretched her long legs. She was half-a-foot taller than petite Chloe.

"Your lasagna is the best." Ava swirled vino, sniffed then sipped.

"It's a recipe I got from the Italian singer. What was his name? He invited us to his place and cooked it when he visited us in New York. It was . . . Hmmm . . . yes . . . Frankie Sinatra."

"Seriously?" Chloe blinked almost spitting a mouthful of wine. "You knew Frank Sinatra . . . and he cooked for you?" Her eyes must've grown wide as the mouth of her goblet.

Angelica smiled casually and pointed to the coffee table. "Please, girls, enjoy the artichoke dip and bagel chips while the main dish finishes baking."

"Gran, don't change the subject. Tell us about Frankie." Chloe stared pointedly. She lay a hand across her mouth, unsure what was real.

"Well certainly, darling; your grandfather and I ran in a well-known crowd. We hung out with movie stars, singers, comedians, politicians and amazingly wicked folks." She chuckled putting a finger to her lips.

"So when you mentioned the Rat Pack, you really knew them?" Puzzle pieces from past chats began to take shape.

"Of course, I did. Why would you question it? I knew many famous celebrities. The spicy redhead—she was smart as a whip. Lucy something—I'll think of it. Her musician husband had escaped Cuba when the Cold War stuff hit the fan. They performed comedy together on a television show. That boy was a typical Latin lover. He'd bed anything with a skirt. He never was good enough for that sweet gal."

"Lucy and Desi Arnaz?" Ava's face was agog as the words slipped out.

"That was it. We danced at the club where Desi played drums—the Copa Cabana. They moved to LA, and we lost track of them."

"Geez, mom, I never heard you talk about them before. I watched their show growing up." Ava's look of shock matched how Chloe felt.

"Yes, Ava, I remember." She patted her daughter's hand adoringly. "What's this I hear about you on the news, Chloe?" Angelica cocked a brow meeting Chloe's eyes.

"There's no need to worry. I hoped you wouldn't hear about it. I was touring houses the other day and found a dead guy in one." Her hand rested on Gran's silky digits.

"I'll be darned if this place isn't getting as dangerous as New York City." Angelica sighed. She leaned into the thick cushions. "People dropped dead left and right when we lived there." She shook her head.

"I wouldn't go that far, Mom. Sweetwater has its share of crime. Murders occur few and far between here, but they're not daily occurrences as in big cities."

"My neighbor said the victim's wife is ranting. Apparently she's accusing his lover of murdering her husband."

"Gran, I didn't realize you tapped into the Sweetwater gossip mill."

"I hear things." Angelica winked.

"You heard right. Mrs. Carnes and Mr. Carnes' girlfriend, Sandy Bennet, are accusing each other." She might as well share what she knew. There was no hiding secrets in this town.

Ava nodded. "I learned at the beauty shop, Sandy was sleeping with Harvey Carnes and he spent money left and right buying her expensive clothing, electronics and jewelry. He must've been raking in the cash to afford it. Sandy threw a hissy prompting their divorce. I heard he was having financial issues, with divorce attorneys digging into his business. I'll bet he was sorry he blew a fortune on his lover. I'm anxious to find out which floozy did the guy in."

Chloe giggled. Wine was getting to her empty stomach fast. "Maybe they're in it together. They could be making a big fuss to confuse authorities." It was a wild idea, but viable.

Angelica and Ava burst into laughter. "That would be a hilarious turn of events." Ava teetered behind a napkin.

"Grandpa never mentioned the man." Angelica studied the ceiling in deep concentration.

"No worries, Mom. The cops can handle it. Speaking of which, I hear Chloe made a new friend. Sadie told me you were at her diner with Deputy Coldwater." Ava's glance moved to Chloe.

Chloe rolled her eyes and smiled. *The Sweetwater mill kept on grinding.* "Yeah, I like Jaiden. She, Casey and I went out a few nights ago." Chloe sat her wine glass down. She should've taken time for lunch and needed food before drinking anything else.

"She's a nice woman. We have a competent bunch on the force," Angelica mused.

Chloe trusted her instincts, but wouldn't mind knowing how her mother felt about Leo. "Deputy Sanders is leading the case, partly because Wyatt has known me all my life. I suspect it's an opportunity for Leo to hone his skills."

"Leo has been with Wyatt about ten years. He's a genuinely good man, kind-hearted, quick to help a neighbor, dependable and easy going. The young man has good genes and even better ethics, born and bred in Sweetwater like his pa and grandpa. You couldn't find a nicer fella. Why do you ask, Chloe? Do I detect interest in our young deputy? It wouldn't be a bad thing." Her mother glanced sideways and winked knowingly.

Was she so easy to read? "I don't know, Mom. I like him, but there's nothing between us. He's professional and pleasant but swamped with work." A gnawing ached in her gut. *If only Leo could change things*. She sipped her wine as a distraction.

"There is a killer loose on our town. It's understandable. This will be over soon, sweetheart. The boy won't be able to ignore your charm forever." Ava smiled with smug satisfied gaze.

What was she up to? "Mom, whatever you're plotting, stay out of it. I'm capable of handling my life."

She patted Chloe's thigh. "Of course you are."

"Dinner's ready." Angelica popped to her feet at the sound of the oven's beep. Angelica served the main dish.

"Great." Chloe sauntered to the bar for a bottle to refill their goblets.

"Let's enjoy at our Sinatra Lasagna. I'll never eat this dish again without hearing the crooner in my head." Chloe chuckled, and the others laughed as she sang, "I did it my way."

CHAPTER 12

Ava made appointments and picked her mother up then retrieved Chloe. They arrived at Doc Maine's office to get physicals before lunch and shopping. Jane Anderson, the receptionist, took Gran to an examination room, deposited Ava in another and Chloe in a third. A nurse made rounds drawing blood, taking blood pressure, temperatures and weight, keying them into a computer.

Ava had discussed concern for her mother with the physician earlier on the phone. So he arranged for special tests to be run on Angelica, to investigate her brain function, running an EKG, a CT scan and general ex-rays. Angelica signed H.E.P.P.A. documents allowing him to divulged health information to Ava and Chloe.

"Okay, Chloe, unless you have something more to discuss, get dressed. I'll finish with your mother then meet the three of you in my office for a chat."

"Thanks, Doc." He left, and Chloe dressed confidant she personally had nothing to worry about. Gran was another story. Then Chloe joined her mother and grandmother in the physician's office.

Regal in white linen slacks and matching button-up shirt, Gran posed with ankles crossed showing off slender feet in white leather flats. "How did it go, sweetheart." She patted the seat beside her, and Chloe took it. Ava sat in the chair to the other side of Angelica.

"It was fine, Gran. How about you?"

"Fit as a fiddle, I'll wager." She smiled patiently gently squeezing Chloe's hand.

"Great."

An impressive desk rested in front of a picture window with a lovely wooded view. Shelves on either side displayed medical journals. Several plaques and framed certificates graced pale blue walls. Dark blue, luxurious carpeting covered the floor. Cozy navy, leather chairs made guests comfortable.

"Doc will be in shortly." Jane poked her head in the door and disappeared.

The elderly physician in a white frock entered. "Thank you, ladies; it's good seeing you today. A fine idea and about time you had physicals. First of all, Ava, I'd like you to follow up with a colonoscopy. There's no specific concern, but you're of an age. We need to keep an eye out in that respect. Also, your blood work shows a slight adjustment needed to control blood pressure. I'll change your prescription. My nurse will phone it to your drug store."

"Thanks, Doc."

"Chloe you're good to go." He linked his fingers and leaned elbows against the desktop gazing at the elder woman. "Angelica, you have concerning issues. Quite frankly your family is worried. I understand you've experienced memory problems."

She blushed sitting even more erect. "I . . . ah . . . I've had a few incidences. Sometimes it's difficult to recall specifics. It's not a continual thing. I'm not foggy brained, but the oddest things completely slip my mind." She glared at Chloe and Ava in turn. Then she smiled regally at her internist. Obviously Gran wasn't pleased they'd discussed her with the doctor.

"What did you eat for breakfast?" He studied her face.

She glanced down and away, as though thinking. "I . . . ah . . ." a gush of air escaped her. She met his eye. "I can't recall breakfast." She glanced at Ava then Chloe and back to the physician looking defeated. "It's the weirdest thing. I ate strawberries with orange juice, champagne, lox and bagels, fresh pastries and grapes for breakfast the day after my wedding; but I can't tell you what I ate three hours ago. Like that, sometimes a mere word slips from my mind—frustrating and embarrassing. I hate it." She grimaced.

"I see. I suspected. We did a hearing test. It indicated you have loss of hearing in your left ear. It can help initiate memory issues and definitely interferes with conversations. You need a hearing aide. We can provide a tiny, inconspicuous one your hair will hide so no one will realize you're wearing it. It will allow you to better communicate."

She seemed apprehensive, and her hands shot up. "I don't know. Hearing aides are for old men." Her hands quivered.

"Angelica, I promise you. No one will be the wiser unless you tell them. Please do this for yourself."

Ava placed a hand on her mother's arm. "Mom, please do it for me. Do it for all of us. You know how frustrating miss-hearing words or not hearing at all can be. You can't talk on the phone because you can't hear well."

"Please, Gran. You need this. Don't deny yourself the ability to hear, especially since it's easily remedied. You'll need to remove it before water aerobics." Chloe joined the argument.

Angelica sighed. Her hands flopped into her lap. "Well, okay, if you insist. It seems I'm outnumbered. If it helps my memory, I'll try it."

125

"It will help you hear and communicate better. That will stimulate your brain and provide an overall more enjoyable lifestyle. Retention is another issue. Tests show you have beginning stages of Alzheimer's disease. Lesions disrupt electrical impulses. The injuries block connections meant to allow the brain to function properly. This irreversible situation starts by effecting memory. We cannot stop it. Parts of the brain die. Dead spots show up on scans. Sometimes these occur due to previous damage from concussions. Sometimes they result from mini-strokes. There are any number reasons one develops the condition."

He flipped on the screen beside him. Angelica's brain scan was displayed. "These lines are the beginnings of the ailment. White spots are dead zones. They aren't wide-spread at this time. As dead spots increase in number, the brain loses control. Eventually it affects, not only memory, but other bodily functions. This incurable malignancy progresses differently in every patient, but it moves forward. You will get worse and no better." He appeared trying to mask sadness on his face.

Tears filled Angelica's eyes, and her hands trembled in her lap. "This will eventually kill me? How long? How long before I don't know who I am—who my family is?" She selected a hanky from her clutch and dabbed her eyes. Then she glanced from Ava to Chloe and back to the man.

Chloe longed to wrap arms around her and sooth her like a baby. Her own heart ached, and her mind kept begging it to prove a bad dream. She reached and clutched the frail, trembling hand. It felt icy.

"There's no way of telling. I'll provide medication to try and slow the process, keep an eye on you, and watch for signs of change." He shoved a brochure to her, and she placed it in her clutch. "Jane will schedule your quarterly exams."

Ava blinked. Tears blurred her vision. Batting her eyes, she dabbed them with a hanky.

"Ava, you and Angelica need to discuss living arrangements. A time will come. Angelica cannot live alone when this progresses. Further down the road, she'll require nursing care."

Ava grabbed her mother's hand and gripped it tightly, giving her a glassy-eyed smile. "We're here for you, Mom—whatever you need—both me and Chloe."

"That's right, Gran. We're sticking together. We can make it through this." Chloe wanted to burst into tears too, but held them at bay with deep breathing. She'd find time to cry. Mom and Gran needed her to keep strong.

They left the office with a schedule of follow up meetings and headed home, each to their own haven, no longer in the mood. Gran's prognosis had soured their stomachs, destroying appetites. Each was distraughtly musing about the revelation.

Gran was abnormally quiet then finally mumbled, "Oh dear, I dread telling Tony. He's so protective. He's got a temper—that one. He's going to have a hemorrhage when I give him my news. I'll be a burden to all of you." Gran's hand quivered.

Patting her mother's shaking hand sympathetically, Ava blinked at tears forming in her eyes. Chloe stalled for breath, trying to understand.

"Mom, Dad's gone a long time. Chloe and I are here for you though. You're a blessing to us—never a burden. We'll see you have the best of care and remain by your side through it. Don't worry about anything."

"Nonsense, I saw Tony . . . ah . . . when was that? Oh yeah, last . . . last Wednesday. We had brunch, and of course sex afterward." She snickered and blushed ducking her head timidly at sharing something so intimate. "He's still a raging bull in the sack."

127

"Geez, Mom, your memory may be getting vague when it comes to the short-term; but you certainly recall long-past events." Ava blushed at the reference to her parents' long-lost sex life.

After settling Angelica into her condo, Ava headed toward Casey's place to drop her off. "I'm worried about her. She's already getting the past mixed with the present. The more time passes, the more she lives in bygone days. Oddly, certain memories are distinct."

"Yeah, it's weird how she acts like things happened recently, when they were actually from when she was young. She remembers Grandpa well. Since you mentioned her issues, I've studied the disease. I found info saying events carrying strong emotional ties out-last others. Hearing her talk about Grandpa is interesting—when she's not describing their sexual exploits. He sounds like a true Italian stud."

"I suppose so. She was quite the stunning woman before I was born, and she moved here. He must've been something special. I don't recall him dating. She's lived alone all these years. Dad must've proved a tough act to follow."

"It's easy seeing how in love she was when she speaks of him. She croons his name sweetly—Tony. It's adorable. I hope to find that kind of deep, devoted love someday."

Leo's face flashed through her mind. Why was him and not Tray? He had pursued her, but Leo had pushed her away. Gran wasn't the only female in the family who was messed up.

"You will, darling. We've got to focus on Mom now, but someone will come into your life when you least expect it."

"I hope you're right. About Gran, her care sounds expensive."

"Dad was successful. I manage her accounts since early last year. She's sitting pretty in cash. Income is deposited monthly into her account from a foundation. I suppose he set it up. She's not too good with accounting or financing. She and a silent partner friend of hers invested a sum in the startup of my real estate company. They get an income from my agency's yearly profit sharing distribution. Over the years Mom accumulated quite a nest egg."

"Good to hear. So that's how you collected enough cash to form your brokerage. I knew it didn't come from Dad. Who is your third financier?" Dad had left them with nothing but a beater vehicle and a large house payment and done nothing since to help either of them.

"I don't know the shareholder's identity. Their profits are deposited into a foundation."

"Doesn't it bother you? I'm curious as hell.

Ava waved a hand and rolled her eyes. "Not in the least. It doesn't concern me. I'm happy having someone involved who stays out of my way and doesn't stick their nose in my everyday affairs. It's probably some old gal from Mom's card club. Most likely she doesn't want the others knowing she's loaded."

Chloe shrugged as Ava entered her driveway. She leaned and kissed Ava's cheek. "Love you, Mom. We'll manage somehow—together. We always do. Gran's money will help. It's undoubtedly going to cost a pretty penny, especially when she needs constant medical attention."

They said their good nights, and Ava drove away.

Chloe wasn't prone to afternoon naps, but once inside alone, she threw herself on her bed and cried until she fell into a deep sleep.

CHAPTER 13

Chloe submitted her bid on the murder house to the listing agent, offering well below asking price due to the circumstances. Discretion being part of their business, the agent didn't flinch when she was asked to keep the deal from Ava. Chloe would break the news to her if the contract was signed.

"No problem, Chloe. I understand. I'd act the same if Ava was my mother. I'll let you know when the widow responds. She's going to probate court today, so should find out when and if she can move forward with a sale soon."

"Thanks, Dottie. I appreciate it."

Chloe's phone rang. Tray's deep, gravelly voice crooned sensually. Chloe's gut fluttered gaily anticipating seeing him. She needed a distraction.

"Meet me at the coffee shop. I'm between jobs and need to grab a bite. I hate to eat alone, but also want to discuss business."

"Sure, I'll leave now." She snatched her briefcase and purse, and headed to meet her client.

Tray was sipping an iced cappuccino and had ordered for her. He waved her over. "Here you go." He stood and held her chair. "Black and dark, the way you like it." He pushed a cup her way.

Her heart flickered. He'd paid attention to her coffee preference, stacking up points left and right. So what if he gave orders. He was used to being the boss, and he was hers. "Thanks, Tray. What's up?"

"I had a lovely time with you the other night. You're a joy to be with. I need you to accompany me today to Lexington. One of my vendors has ideas to present which might affect pricing on units you're selling. I want your perspective. You know better than they, how the market will react to specific aspects of homes." The dude was persuasive, though he expected her to jump without a moment's notice.

She had hoped to finish a ton of marketing paperwork during the afternoon. That could wait. It was difficult conjuring up a viable excuse to refuse. "Sure, it sounds doable."

He was better than Chloe at keeping business separate from pleasure. Their dinner date hadn't seemed like business. They had avoided talk about real estate, and enjoyed an intimate goodnight. She'd considered it a date.

Tray's glossy smile and a twinkle in his eyes engaged cute dimples in his square jaws. The man knew how to turn on charm and use stunning looks to get his way.

Damn, he flirts well.

"My ulterior motive is convincing you to attend the ballet. Let me take you to the finest steak house Lexington has to offer. We'll return home rather late. If you prefer, we can sleep over at a hotel." His eloquent attempt to look coy and boyish was merely surface gloss. The man knew exactly what he was doing. He was an expert manipulator.

Her face flushed hot, and she glanced away. Using business to snare another date wasn't surprising. Spending the night with Tray was another story. It was way too soon.

He acted flustered and awkward. It resembled pretense. She was sure he was feeling her out, seeing how far she'd go, and didn't want her to realize it—but she saw through his charade.

"No worries, Chloe. I'll arrange separate rooms, of course."

Yeah, right. Nice follow through.

All the charm in the world and Tray was a typical guy. Men wanted to see how long it would take to get a gal in the sack.

What the heck?

She didn't have other plans. Might as well partake of what was available. It made no difference to her if he wanted to combine pleasure with a business. She could stand her ground.

"Of course, dinner and a ballet sound fine. I need to make the long drive back to Sweetwater tonight. I have a lot to do, and don't want a late start tomorrow. I'll run by my house before we leave to pick up a gown suitable for the opera." She almost smelled disappointment oozing from his pores.

Clearly women didn't often say no to Mr. Ackerson. "Whatever works best is no problem for me."

She liked Tray, but something held her back and wasn't ready for a sleepover with the handsome stud. He played at manipulation a bit too much for comfort. He'd have to take it at her pace, or walk away—that simple.

Leo Sanders stepped into the crowded coffee shop and glared their direction. His eyes burned scaling across her face—clearly none too pleased seeing her with Tray.

133

Too bad. He'd left her hanging. *What did he expect?* Besides, Tray was a business associate.

Leo's seething glare settled on Tray. Without approaching the counter to order, he stalked to their table. Standing feet shoulder-width apart and hands on his utility belt, he scowled down his nose. Barely glancing Chloe's direction, he nodded without meeting her gaze.

His voice was soft as he said, "Chloe."

He glared at Tray. "What's with you, Ackerson? I've called your office three times. They keep telling me you'd stop by the station. You've yet to make an appearance. Must I cuff you and drag your ass in for interrogation?"

"Back off, Sanders; no need to hassle me unduly. I'll speak with my attorney today about harassment. Stop interfering with my business. I'll get to your damned station in due time, and answer whatever petty questions you've come up with to screw with me. I've got nothing to do with your murder case, anyway. You have no call bothering me. Now leave us alone. You're embarrassing yourself." Tray grimaced around taking in the nosy clientele.

Chloe's face heated, and hair stood on end. Their behavior was odd. Did these guys know each other? They acted too familiar and pissed to be strangers. She resisted the urge to flee or climb beneath the tiny table, wishing she was anywhere but here.

Leo stood straighter with shoulders back, scrutinizing his opponent. "I resent your attitude, Ackerson. Who do you think you are? No one's above the law. There's a link to you in my case. If you want your name cleared, you'd best comply. You're coming in one way or another. Show up before three today, or I'll arrest you, and you can spend a night in my cell." Leo spun and stomped out without getting whatever he'd come for.

Tray shook his head acting disgusted. "I apologize for the scene, Chloe. Deputy Sanders has a personal vendetta.

He's using his investigation to rile me. I'm sorry we made you uncomfortable." He reached for her hand, but his attempt to brush off the incident as insignificant fell flat.

She allowed him to hold it for a second. His palm was hot and wet, and his pulse beat strong and fast. She eased from his grasp, reaching for her purse. The sweet sensation from his touch she'd previously experienced had disappeared.

Her gut said he was trying to influence her impression. Apprehension set in. She needed space. "Listen, Tray, whatever is going on between you and Leo is your affair. It has nothing to do with me. You have this police thing to clear up. Can we move our Lexington excursion to tomorrow and skip the ballet?" She stood ready to leave. She wasn't going out with Tray again unless things cleared up and anxiety about him disappeared.

Disappointment played in his eyes. "Certainly, whatever you want. Our meeting with the Foundation Corporation can wait until tomorrow. I'll get rid of Sanders today. I'm sorry we'll miss the ballet. I was looking forward to spending the evening with you. We can still do dinner." He ran a hand down her forearm.

If he was dragging her all the way to Lexington, the least he could do was feed her. She didn't want to go to the damned ballet anyway.

Instead of a thrill she shivered at contact. He smiled seemingly taking her response as a positive reaction and winked. "I'll return you to Sweetwater before evening."

Damned right you will.

"Perfect." She picked up her go-cup and spun to leave. "I've got to run—got another appointment."

Yeah, sure; I'll work on it.

At first mention, the ballet had sounded like an appealing excuse to hold Tray's hand in the dark. Suddenly the idea of being in the dark with him made her insides shiver.

Leo's attitude sent warning signals flashing in her, enough to warrant stepping back from a romantic relationship. No sense rushing things. Tray wasn't going anywhere. She needed to figure the lay of the land before choosing a trail.

Something weird was brewing between the men. She needed to get to the bottom of it.

After work Chloe waited in the cashier's line to pay for groceries. Leo's head spanned the store preoccupied, obviously trying to determine if he'd forgotten anything. He absentmindedly made his way through the front of the store and pulled in behind her.

His cart was filled with fresh fruit, hot dogs, pizza rolls, milk, and a box of those kiddy yogurts you suck instead of eating with a spoon. Precariously balanced atop a pile of bread, cookies and crackers sat a sippy cup with green tractors on it.

"Hey, Leo, interesting load you've got there. You eat like a kid." She chuckled perusing his cart of child-friendly foods. She lifted the cup. "And you drink like one, too." He probably bought it for a friend.

His face reddened. An anxious expression crossed it, quickly replaced by resolution. "Chloe, I meant to tell you. I'd have gotten around to telling you I've got a young one when I meet an interesting woman."

"Tell me?" He was interested in her. *Yeah.*

"My son, Cy's almost four. My wife, Claire died when Cy was a few months old. I'm a single dad." His eyes were wide, as though studying her expression while he blurted out the explanation awkwardly.

Her head numbed. Her chest froze, refusing air, and her mouth hung open. "I . . . ah . . . I didn't know." She stammered. "I'm . . . I . . . ah . . . I'm sorry for your loss."

Why the hell didn't Casey tell her—or Mom? Surely they were aware.

He fumbled with a grocery list, wadding it nervously in his hands. "Leading with 'hey, I'm a dad' turns most women off. I like you and didn't want you running for the hills before we got to know each other. I would've told you . . . soon."

The shopper in front moved away, and the cashier began scanning Chloe's items. She moved to the pay station for a distraction from Leo's revelation. She hadn't pictured him as a grieving widower, or as a man with a family.

Is this what Mom meant by responsible?

Jaiden and Casey had also used that word describing him.

Why the hell didn't someone tell me?

"I'm sorry you found out this way." His hand shook placing purchases on the conveyor belt. "Please, don't get mad."

Feeling tossed from a saddle, she faced him with hands on hips and tilted head. Scrutinizing from top down, she met his pleading eyes. Mercy began sputtering to life within her. She liked him too. How would she have responded if she knew from the beginning?

"I'm not mad, Leo. I'm disappointed. You didn't think I could handle you having a life before we met. You aren't the only person with baggage. My closet is full of skeletons. I could tell you things about me that might send you racing away. Everybody has a past. Get over yourself." She paid for groceries ignoring him.

"Chloe, I meant what I said. I like you. I want to continue seeing you."

137

She pushed her cart out of his way. He moved up.

She glared at the man she hadn't even begun seeing yet. "Continue? That so? I'm not so sure. I'm discovering sides of you that make me wonder."

It wouldn't hurt him to stammer a while longer. She'd certainly had enough time to stew thinking about him. He owed her an explanation for his behavior.

Ignoring the cashier, he stepped close to Chloe. A whiff of aftershave teased her nostrils. They locked eyes. The sparkle made her wonder what was running through his mind. His hands rested on her shoulders. She resisted the urge to shrug them off. The closeness felt too good.

"I'm sorry you got thrown in the middle of my tiff with Ackerson. Something clicks in me when I'm around the dude. Being close to the man is hazardous. Watch yourself with him. He's not what he seems. His fancy, polished exterior hides a shady side. Be wary." His voice barely above a whisper, gentle warmth of his breath filtered over her face making her want to lean into him, and seek out those luscious lips in a tender kiss.

No time for day dreaming. She'd best stick with reality.

"You knew Tray before he moved here?" A dark mood began festering inside her. She usually listened to her subconscious mind's warnings. Was Leo correct about Tray? Or was he simply envious? She wasn't sure.

"You're acting like a jealous teenager."

"It's not about you, but I worry you're spending time with him. Seriously, Chloe, he's bad news. There are things you don't know. Don't fall under his spell. Watch yourself."

"Leo, I can take care of myself. Tray Ackerson is a business associate . . . and a friend. I don't appreciate you bad-mouthing him."

When he didn't elaborate in a couple seconds, she spun and shoved her cart toward the exit. No call for Leo to act prissy about her being with Tray. Who she saw socially and worked with was none of his business. He wanted to spend time with her, but made no move to see it through. When the hell was that going to happen? Leo might be all talk and no follow through.

She was a free agent. She hadn't committed exclusively, or any way to any man—since Hal. If only the sexy deputy didn't make her heart flutter.

CHAPTER 14

Chloe and Jaiden met for drinks at The Ten Mile House. After going the rounds talking with customers and friends and purchasing beers from Justin at the bar, they settled into a table far from the juke box. George Strait crooned about lost love. Patrons chatted among themselves.

"How's it going? Hear anything about the house?" Jaiden studied her expression sipping the cool beverage.

"I submitted the offer. With the estate in probate, the widow can't officially enter a contract to sell until she is granted the right to do so. I'm hoping no one submits an offer while I'm waiting."

Jaiden looked at her beneath her brows and patted the top of her hand. "Hon, no one is going to bid against you for a house that someone was recently murdered in."

"You're probably right." Anxious and jittery, not merely about the house, she didn't want to ruin her friendship with Jaiden, but hopefully she'd shed insight about Leo's confusing behavior. "Any news on the case?" The sooner solved the better for everyone, including Chloe.

"Nah, nothing definitive; we're following money trails. They're leading to surprising events. Are you and Leo dating, since you've been cleared?"

Chloe shrugged and breathed a sigh of relief. "No, he hasn't called or asked me out. We had a date scheduled, but he cancelled when the investigation began. He doesn't have time for me."

"He's pretty busy and working a lot of hours. No worries, he'll find time." Jaiden relaxed into her chair.

Her words brought a measure of comfort. "I like Leo, but he's acting strangely. I ran into him shopping today. He was buying food for a kid. I jokingly called him on it, thinking he was picking stuff up for a friend. He admitted having a son. It stung that he didn't want to confide in me until we knew each other better. He said he wants to see me more, but I'm not confident he'll call."

Jaiden eyed her curiously. "Why on earth not? You'd be good for each other. I can't imagine you the type turned off by a kid, especially one adorable as Cy. You think his daddy's cute? Wait until you get a load of the little guy. He's a perfect, toy doll—cute as a new born colt and sweet like honeysuckle." Her face softened with a smile.

"That's nice. I can't wait to meet the little tyke. I can't imagine being a lone parent of a small boy. It sounds like a huge job." Leo was a stand-up guy and honorable man who'd take responsibility seriously. The way his eyes shown when he spoke Cy's name, it was obvious he adored the boy. She'd wager he was a good dad—unlike her own.

Jaiden nodded with brows rising and falling. "I'd say, but Leo's up to it. He's proud of young Cy and crazy in love with the kid. He took Claire's death hard. Soon after I moved to town I got to know them. She became sick, and it was over before we knew what was what. Leo hasn't dated much. He and Casey actually dated a couple times."

"Yeah, Casey told me. It didn't work out. They're too much alike." She'd never pursue Leo if Casey cared for him.

"They're better as buddies." Jaiden swigged her beer.

"Clair's a pretty name. I keep trying to picture Leo married. I had him figured or a bachelor through and through." He was full of delightful surprises.

"Nope, our boy works hard and spends his down time with his son. His mom helps out while he works. He has a part-time nanny, too. It's tough, especially with a baby; but he's come through for the child. I admire him. Don't you?" Jaiden nodded, evaluating her answer.

"Well, yeah; it's admirable. I wish I'd known sooner. I'm seeing a different side of Leo. There's something else that's bothering me. Maybe you can help." Hopefully she wouldn't turn her new buddy off by asking the favor. She didn't want Jaiden thinking she was a gossip.

Jaiden sat straight, elbows on the table; and hands surrounding her sweaty, amber bottle. "What's up?"

"I'm seeing this other guy, too." *Did I detect a momentary wince or imagination it?* "I sold Tray Ackerson a home and listed his subdivision for sale. We went out once, and he's asked me out again today. We cancelled because Leo pitched a hissy in public about Tray coming in immediately for questioning."

"Tray Ackerson?" No mistaking her grimace. Maybe it wasn't about gossiping or her playing the field. She looked none too pleased about the man.

"Yes, that's him. What's between those two? They act like they know each other, but neither is forthcoming with explanation. They looked like two stallions kicking and bucking over a filly in heat. I don't believe it was about me—not entirely, anyway." She peeled strips the label from her bottle, watching Jaiden sideways.

"Financials in the case file indicate there's a link between Tray Ackerson and the company Harvey Carnes worked for. A press release went out about it, so it was okay to share."

143

"Yes. The Foundation Corporation is a vendor Tray hires to construct foundations for his developments. He purchases raw materials through them." What did that have to do with Carnes?

"Ackerson didn't tell you he's part-owner?" Jaiden's brow rose then fell.

Chloe bit the side of her lip. Her gut feeling about Tray was growing stronger. He was hiding something. Was it none of her business or could it be pertinent? She needed to find out.

"He didn't mention it. Of course, he's wealthy with lots of connections. He hasn't divulged his complete financial structure to me. Why would he—none of my business?"

"Let's say the company has shady ownership with questionable background and practices that need clarified. Tray's a silent partner. He does business with seedy characters. Things may not prove on the up-and-up with Tray Ackerson. I'd watch my step with the guy."

Jaiden's warning sent a chill down Chloe's spine. "Thanks for sharing. Leo gave me the same warning. I'll keep my eyes opened for off-color business activity. Everything I've seen so far looks legitimate. There's something else I wanted to ask you about. The confrontation between Leo and Tray had strong personal undertones. Something nasty is brewing between them aside from the case. I thought you suspected the wife or girlfriend. Is Tray a suspect now?"

"We did. Both gals are volatile and unpredictable, but they had clear alibis. They're still at odds with each other. I hope they stay the hell apart, out of trouble, and let the fury in them die down. We've got other things to worry about. I'm not sure about a personal link between Ackerson and Leo. I'll look into it. We're delving into several oddities at the company. The CEO provided access to corporate financials, and something seems amiss. An auditor is sifting through them now. We're questioning staff—folks Harvey would've had contact with at work."

"Sounds complicated; you've got tons of work to do to solve the crime. Thanks for checking into Leo and Tray's connection. They acted downright hostile. I'd really like to know what's up with them."

"No problem. Since they threw you in the middle of their spat, you've got a right to question their behavior. Unless it's something confidential, I'll let you know what I find out."

♥♥♥♥

Jaiden cornered Leo in the breakroom the next morning. From the expression on her face, she wasn't interested in work. "What's on your agenda today?"

"I'm heading to Lexington to talk with the construction folks. Want to join?" He appreciated her take on things. She was a valuable asset to the force.

"Sure, I'll ride along. I wanted to ask you about something. I had drinks last night with Chloe. She's concerned about your attitude with Tray Ackerson. She said you two acted like a couple studs squaring off yesterday. She got the feeling there's a personal tiff between you. She is worried about you. She's also confused. She's doing business and has a personal friendship with Mr. Ackerson."

He shook his head and blinked, hands on hips. He'd shoved Chloe into the middle of his beef with the pompous asshole. Now he had explaining to do. "Damn. I wish she'd keep away from the dude. He's bad news. I don't want her hurt."

"She can't exactly walk away from his business. She listed his properties for sale, so she works for him. Starting over in Sweetwater, I'd wager she needs the deals."

"I hate it." Why'd the money-bagged loudmouth move to Sweetwater anyway? Leo needed to get to the bottom of it. He suspected it had to do with Tray's ties to the ex-mobster partner. Chloe mentioned a business associate had recommended Tray. He'd lay odds it was Rizzo—but *why would he even know Chloe Roberts existed*?

"What's the deal with Ackerson? Do you know him personally?" Jaiden propped her butt against the counter, cradled her coffee cup, and crossed her ankles. She clearly signaled—they were going nowhere without explanation. She was a dog with a bone sinking her teeth into something. He might as well fess up.

"Ackerson resided in New York but one of his partners, Anthony Rizzo moved to Lexington years ago. Rizzo started the Foundation Corporation. Claire was engaged to Ackerson. She lived in Lexington when we met. Ackerson blames me for their breakup." He never should've confronted Ackerson with Chloe around.

"I'm sorry you're going through this with him. Is he wrong, or did you break them up? You've suffered enough, losing Claire that way."

He hated Jaiden feeling sorry for him. "No, Claire broke up with him because when she grew to know him she didn't trust him."

"I get that you're trying to protect Chloe. But she doesn't understand. Chloe didn't even know you were a widower. Give her a break. She likes you. If you care for her at all, she needs to trust you. Level with her about yourself." Her hands clasped the hot beverage. A long, red nail pointed his direction accusingly.

The gnawing sense he'd screwed something beautiful up rumbled in his gut. "You're right. I need to be straight with Chloe. I was afraid to tell her about Cy. A lot of women are turned off by a single dad." Dreaded loneliness edged its way into his mood. He shrugged it off. He had work to do and needed to find a way to make peace with Chloe.

"I can see how it could. But Chloe likes you. She's got a past, too. She can handle it. Be open with her, if you want a chance with her."

"You're right. I'll try to fix it. I want to keep seeing her."

If she's willing.

"Don't you have some time scheduled off soon?" Jaiden winked then strolled from the breakroom.

Not a bad idea. He made a quick call to his mom. She could keep Cy for a couple hours on his day off. He rang Chloe's cell.

"Hey." His voice sounded timid.

"Hi, Leo. What's up?" Wariness tinged her voice.

At least she didn't hang up. A good sign.

"You free for a couple hours day after tomorrow? I have that day off. We could go riding. We need to talk." Last time he was this anxious he had been a senior asking popular Sara Jane Smith to the prom. The long hesitation on Chloe's end did nothing to help his nerves. He inhaled deeply giving her time.

"I'd love it, Leo. You have a mount for me? What time?"

He hoped it was a glint of excitement he detected in her voice. "Sure do. I board at the Henderson farm. Justin has a fine ride. She probably needs exercising. He'd appreciate you riding her. I'll pick you up at nine."

"Okay, see you then." She clicked off. He liked a woman who didn't waste words.

CHAPTER 15

Tray and Chloe joined Anthony Rizzo in the large Foundation Corporation conference room. A couple managers in charge of product supply strolled in and took seats along one side. Chloe sat to Tray's right as far away from Rizzo as possible.

She was yet unclear why she was an asset to this meeting. Tray likely wanted her to attend for the opportunity to wine and dine her again. It wasn't about to happen. She might let him feed her, but it would be about business, and not personal.

The hour and half drive to Lexington filled with discussion of Tray's subdivision, had whittled the edge off of Chloe's nervousness about the trip. She'd continually made notes on her laptop, capturing details he spouted. He hadn't mentioned their canceled opera date or the night he'd brought flowers and they'd enjoyed a more intimate time together, though she was sure he'd felt something for her that evening.

But was she? She knew little about the man who was an enigma—a master manipulator. She wouldn't actually call it deception, but he donned whatever front he wanted someone to see.

Rizzo and his men suggested ideas for cost savings in a presentation. The proposal was over Chloe's head. She listened patiently trying to pinpoint areas she could assist Tray. It was, after all, why he brought her along.

Yeah, sure.

Something bugged her about the elegantly clad CEO. They'd never met, but he seemed vaguely familiar.

Personifying Italian descent, suave and debonair in an old-worldly fashion, Anthony Rizzo must've been a hit with the gals in his younger days. He'd aged well. Probably in his eighties. A thick, silver mane sported traces of jet-black around the temples. He moved with confidence and grace gained from years of command.

Rizzo explained the meeting's purpose. Apparently they had concocted options to provide additional luxury specs in Tray's housing without adding mega cost to the budget.

After brief introductions, Coy James did most of the talking. His unimpressive, slim body packed into an off-the-rack, blue, linen suit. His manner rubbed Chloe the wrong way, but she couldn't pinpoint why. The habit of continually fingering thick spectacles into place was getting on her last nerve.

Finally he turned the slide show over to his assistant, Ben Thurman. Ben's cheap, knockoff, brown suit washed out his already pallid complexion. Short and stubby, his belly strained against a leather belt barely holding it in. He directed attention to visuals, speaking and pointing stubby fingers with nails chewed unevenly to the quick. His hands trembled slightly manipulating the screen, obviously not accustomed to the spotlight.

A knock at the door, and Rizzo's attractive secretary, Katy, entered timidly. "Mr. Rizzo, I'm sorry to interrupt your meeting. It's extremely important."

Acting perplexed, he appeared to be hiding irritation. He trod toward the exit, and stood close to Katy as she whispered, but in the tight space Chloe heard.

"The police wish to see you. They want to talk first with you, then Mr. James, Mr. Thurman and everyone who worked with Harvey Carnes."

Rizzo rolled his eyes and turned, appearing resolved. "It is okay, Katy. Please, see the officers in. I have nothing to hide. It's an inconvenient time, but we'll do what we can to help. They can use this room. Please tell the staff, no one goes to lunch until released by the investigators."

Returning to his seat regally, he spread his broad hands on the tabletop. "Tray, unfortunately we need to call this to a halt. The team has provided sufficient data. Take the packets they passed out. Study it. I'll be in touch soon to get your decision."

Chloe and Tray were dismissed. Rizzo's men acted extremely nervous. They blanched more than their normal ashen hues as they left. She understood being target of such an investigation, so shrugged it off.

Tray picked up the packet. The officers entered. Chloe hung out beside him afraid to breathe when a chill filled the air.

Geez.

Leo and Jaiden entered the room, followed by Katy. Jaiden nodded and smiled. Leo grazed at her with an expression anything but pleasant. His jaw tightened, and his harsh squint remained. Chloe wanted to crawl beneath the table and hide. Leo blinked a couple of times then glared at Tray before paying attention to the CEO.

"Mr. Rizzo, meet Sweetwater Deputies Leo Sanders and Jaiden Coldwater." Katy backed out of the conference room shutting the door.

"I'm sorry to interrupt business, Mr. Rizzo, Ackerson and Ms. Roberts. It is imperative we speak with Foundation Corporation employees today."

151

"No worries." Tray shrugged half-heartedly slipping his hands into his jacket pockets. He moved slow and steady, keeping a keen eye on Leo's face. "We're done here. Ms. Roberts and I will enjoy an early lunch, now that we have the afternoon free." He stared Leo in the eye without expression, daring him to comment.

"Ackerson, we'll set up additional time to chat with you again. There's a new line of investigation you can shed light on. I'll contact you in a couple days. Don't leave town without consulting me or the sheriff." Leo stood erect with shoulders back and moved with clenched muscles. His hands slipped into his pants pockets, mirroring Tray's movement. His eyes stayed locked on Trays. His jaw was set.

Tray put a hand to Chloe's back, and she followed him to the door. It was firm and cool, but felt mechanical, not personal. Leo curtly nodded.

"No doubt." Tray's eyes narrowed frowning at the lawman. He rubbed the back of his neck. With a light touch he ushered her out.

His voice rose with a forced smile. "Let's try the restaurant we talked about, Chloe." His attempt to sound upbeat came across strained. Glancing back, his tone resonated louder than normal. Obviously he wanted Leo to hear. "Sanders, you know how to reach me." He shut the door with a snap.

Leo had acted shocked and disappointed seeing her with Tray.

She didn't speak until they reached the restaurant, fearing her voice would quake from nervousness. Tray kept quiet, obviously dealing with demons of his own.

What was with those two? They acted like two steeds ready to duke it out over an in-season mare.

CHAPTER 16

Jaiden called her later that night. "Man, what an uncomfortable day. I knew you did business with Ackerson, but finding you with him in Rizzo's office was a shocker."

"Yeah, I've always been good with timing. We'd scheduled the meeting the day before. I didn't know how to get out of it, but was sorry I attended. I wasn't of help anyway. Besides, the trip was to influence me to go out with him again."

"Yeah, he made that clear. Leo almost swallowed his tongue. How was your early dinner?"

"Dinner and the drive home were strained. He was preoccupied with the way things wit Rizzo, and I was pissed at Tray's smart ass attempt to convince Leo it wasn't a business meal. Why would Tray care if I date Leo. I'm not committed to anyone. One date doesn't mean anything, though Leo will probably cancel our date tomorrow because of it. I wish I understood what is wrong between those two melon heads."

"I don't know. Give Leo a chance. You could be wrong. Is Ackerson okay with you?"

"Who knows? He has issues with Leo I don't understand. It's beginning to boil my blood." She made a fist. "He wasn't satisfied with the vendor's presentation, and I can't tell if he is unhappy with me or not. I've done everything in my power to please him as as customer and have put considerable hours in on the project. Surely he won't pull his real estate listings. He wants them well advertised and sold quickly and efficiently. I've done what needs to be done for that to happen, and I'm eager to sell them and reap the commission. How did your visit go?"

"Rizzo gave our auditor access to company accounts. I don't know yet what is going on; however, a line of funds from the Foundation Corporation flows into an off-shore account in Tray's name. Each time he pays a bill, they divert part of it into the shady account. It appears suspicious, but could prove to be innocent. A holding company in his name is part owner of the corporation. He's in bed with Anthony Rizzo in more ways than one. Watch yourself with those guys. Rizzo's got a sinister reputation." Jaiden's eerie tone sent chills down Chloe's spine.

She'd instantly suspected a strong tie between the men when she witnessed them together. They acted extremely familiar, more than simply vendor and customer. Of course, Mr. Rizzo had eyed her strangely, as well. Maybe it was his normal manner, but it put her on edge.

"Leo told me about Tray's link to C.F. This is the first I've heard about Anthony Rizzo. Tell me more." Even if he was strange, the man was class and charm rolled into a fine suit and well-stacked body for a guy his age.

"His company is legit—this one at least. He's part owner in Entertainment Masters, a gambling consortium based in New York. E.M. owns casinos across the nation and a handful in Las Vegas. Rumor has it the group was formed as a legal outfit by the New York Syndicate when they were forced out of illegal gambling in the seventies. Rizzo has past ties to criminal activity. We think he moved to Lexington to manage their latest ventures. I understand he was a gangster with high standings. Be wary of him."

"Are you saying Entertainment Masters is managed by ex-mobsters? Hal worked form them in New York." Life drained from her head, and she swooned. She plunked into her chair like a balloon losing air. "Don't tell me Hal was mixed up with criminals. Did it have something to do with his disappearance?"

"Honey child, I can't tell you that. I have no clue. The board of directors is made up of suspected ex-gang men—including Anthony Rizzo. Some served time. Others, like Rizzo, were never successfully convicted."

"Tray is one of these guys? Damn." Words gushed out with her last breath of air.

"Not sure. Tray's much younger, and was probably a kid when the Mob was openly powerful. Far as we know, the Lexington business and Tray's development company are legitimate. We haven't uncovered evidence proving otherwise—yet. In the meantime I wanted to share enough with you so you'll watch your step. Leo was right to warn you."

She adjusted her position and rubbed her leg nervously. "What did you find out about Leo?"

"He has reason to be angry with Tray. Tray has a personal vendetta with Leo, but he's under a wrong assumption. I'd steer clear of that, if I were you; but if you want to know more, ask Leo. He's got explaining to do where you're concerned."

Her friend brought some relief, but established new concerns for Chloe. "Jaiden, you're a true pal, and I appreciate you sharing. I understand. You're Leo's friend also, and must keep his confidence. Thanks for your help."

"No worries. Enjoy your date with our esteemed Deputy Sanders. Play nice." Her teasing lilt helped boost Chloe's spirits.

"Sure thing. Bye."

They disconnected.

♥♥♥♥

Chloe tucked her shirt in and zipped her jeans then stepped into her favorite, worn boots. The doorbell rang. Casey was already at the hospital, so she grabbed her cowboy hat from the bed frame and ran down the hallway to the front door.

Snapping it opened sunshine filtered in; its rays almost as welcome as those shining from Leo. His irresistible smile engaged every muscle in his face, creasing outer edges of twinkling jade eyes. He didn't look angry.

She breathed a sigh of relief. "Morning, Leo." Chloe spun around and bent over retrieving her purse from the floor. She whipped back around.

Leo was in a dead stare, ogling her behind. It was impossible to miss his stop-sign-red color. He blinked and glanced away, realizing he was caught him.

He cleared his throat and held the door open for her. "Morning, Chloe. I'm glad you ride and were able to join me. It's one of my favorite past times."

She stepped into the warm, sunlit day to the tune of birds chattering wildly, as they gathered straw and constructed nests for their eggs. "I love spring. The world comes alive, and everything is renewed. It's the perfect weather for riding. Thanks for inviting me. Its years since I've been on horseback. Of course, no one grows up in Sweetwater without learning to ride horses. This community thrives on the equestrian industry."

He led her to his pickup truck with a hand grazing the base of her spine. Her heart did a happy dance at his touch. His strong hands gripped her waist and hoisted her into the tall cab as though she was weightless. The touch left a lasting fiery imprint through thin fabric of her shirt. He raced around and climbed in beside her, giving her time to catch her breath.

On route to the Henderson farm they chatted cordially about weather, work and their mothers, avoiding discussion of the previous day, Tray Ackerson, and Leo's deception about Cy.

He parked outside the ancient wooden barn that had been repaired and gotten a fresh coat of paint. They walked into the breezeway, and Leo flipped lights on. Two horses whinnied, sticking their heads out above stall doors.

Leo spoke softly to the animals, as he opened the doors and attached lead ropes to their halters. Then he led them into the fairway and tied them to large metal rings attached to the wall.

He led her into a small, organized tack room, where he picked up gear and nodded at a set sitting on a wall-attached saddle rack. "You'll borrow Corrie's extra set." He hefted his load and carried it toward where the horses were hitched.

She followed suit carrying the one he'd pointed out. First she slipped the blanket over her steed's back and plopped the saddle atop it.

Looking over his gelding's backside, he grinned with approval. "I would've carried it for you."

"It's okay. I don't mind. It wasn't too heavy." It was nice knowing her cowboy deputy was a gentleman. She straightened the equipment and went about tacking up her mare, as did Leo.

"Corrie is at Adelle Industries in New York. As CEO, she can't miss a board meeting. Her daughter Madison is in class at the high school. Justin is stocking inventory at the Ten Mile House. So no one's around. Justin said to make ourselves at home."

159

"They don't mind if we come and go as we please?" She was uncomfortable traipsing around someone's property.

"Not at all; I have an arrangement with Justin. I ride whenever I want, which isn't often enough. I'm free to use Jazzabelle if I bring a guest. She doesn't get ridden enough, and Zorro loves her. Justin knew we were coming, so he caught them and stalled them for us before he left for work."

"That's fantastic of him. I like the Hendersons. They make a great couple."

"Yeah, they've known each other their whole lives but only got together a couple years back. They sure act happy."

"Doesn't Morgan resent her mom's new husband? Her dad's in New York. Right?"

She was curious about the unusual couple from drastically different social circles, having observed them at the bar. When she was around, the wealthy heiress served customers alongside her handsome, slightly limping bartender husband.

"Lane Parrish is a player, a son-of-a-bitch, not much of a father. He screwed around on Corrie in public. She divorced him when Morgan got old enough to care about photos in the paper of her dad with strange women. Moving here after Corrie's divorce, Morgan was pissed at first. She bonded with Justin before Corrie and he got together. He's become the father figure she needed and didn't get in her own. Apparently, Lane Parrish cares for no one but himself—not even his daughter."

It was reassuring how he didn't condone Mr. Parrish's cheating, and he sounded sympathetic toward the frustrated teen. Leo Sanders would make someone a fine husband. He was a true family man, and Chloe envied that.

"Too bad, but I can relate. After Mom and Dad divorced, he married a young plaything, and his priority is his new family. I don't exist any longer. It burns Mom, his new wife is almost my age." The emptiness she experienced thinking of Dad swarmed her belly. She gave the cinch a last jerk in lieu of hitting something. Jazz expelled a huff of air, and Chloe buckled it tight. She stroked Jazz's mane. "Sorry, girl." She untied the lead rope.

"He doesn't live here. Does he?" Leo secured loaded saddlebags on the rear of his seat.

"No, they moved to Tampa. I'm glad." She flopped the fender down and stepped a booted foot into the stirrup. Raising her body holding onto Jazz's mane, she jumped into the foothold and swung her other leg. The high-backed western saddle sat comfortably.

Leo swung onto Zorro and rode out the barn. Jazzabelle trotted forward taking lead. She walked through the gate into a pasture.

"Is this the right direction?" She spoke loudly, so Leo could hear as he trailed.

"Yeah, it's fine. Jazz likes leading, like most mares. She knows the trail around the farm. Zorro enjoys being behind where he can sniff her rear. If we get to a turning point, I'll let you know. Stick close to the edge, so we don't trod on Justin's hayfield flat."

She giggled. "It's funny how geldings act with mares, though they can't do anything about it. He's hopelessly in lust with Jazz, I see."

She liked having the soft-tempered country boy following her. There might be something to this mare thing. She chuckled, wondering if Leo was fascinated with the view of her butt.

They rode around lush fields brimming with thick Kentucky bluegrass and over small hills full of spring flowers. Trails were easy to see; and true to Leo's words, Jazz knew where she was going; so Chloe gave the girl her head. Occasionally Leo stopped to open and shut gates as they moved from one pasture to another. Eventually they rode into a stand of thick woodlands.

A clearing beside a sparking pond revealed a hideaway surrounded by thick hardwood occupied by a hand-carved bench glossed to shine. A message of love had been carved into the seat. Chloe blushed feeling she was intruding on an intimate interlude.

"Justin built it for Corrie. She's a jogger and runs these trails every morning. He surprised her with it when he asked her to marry him." He led Zorro into the edge of the pond so he could lap water.

Chloe urged Jazz to the bank and allowed her to take step into the muck. Her glossy, blond mane bent forward, and she drank loudly slurping. She wadded knuckle deep and began splashing with her hoof. Water sprayed wetting her belly. Chloe squealed and jerked her feet from the stirrups, sticking legs out and attempting to avoid the deluge.

"Yikes, she's a water dog." She giggled.

Zorro walked deeper in and joined the fun. Leo did the same with his feet, allowing the animal sufficient splashing to cool himself. Then he lightly yanked the reins to the side. Zorro headed up the bank, and Jazz followed.

"They both are. You have to admit it was refreshing." He glanced at his damp jeans and boots, having reacted slower than Chloe.

"I see the attraction. I was hot too." She wiped sweat from her brow with the back of her hand.

Leo sidled beside her, twisted and opened the saddlebag. He whisked out two cold bottles of water. "Here you go. Drink up. I'll carry the empties in the saddlebag when you're done." He cracked one open and handed it to her.

"Thanks." She sipped heartily consuming a third of the refreshing fluid. "Water never tasted so good."

"No problem. I'm glad you came today. I had fun and enjoy your company. I like you, Chloe. I owe you an apology for not being up front about my situation. I'm used to women turning away hearing I have a child. I was afraid to say anything until we got better acquainted. It was stupid of me, and I'm sorry."

"I've forgiven you, Leo. No worries, and I understand. Rest assured I'm not running because you have responsibilities. I adore children and want my own someday." If Hal hadn't disappeared, she'd probably be married and have a baby by now.

Usual emptiness and angst she felt thinking about Hal had lessened, though she continued to miss him. Wondering what might have happened had he not disappeared was useless. At least pain and grief had waned with time. Maybe there was something about the closure exercise Casey made her do. It didn't matter, and she may never know. One thing for certain, being with Leo helped.

"Cy's a great kid. He's affectionate, smart, cute and well-behaved. He's the most adorable child in Sweetwater." Leo blushed. Pride was evident in his tone, and his chest shot out and shoulders rocked back. A gleam showed in his eyes. She liked this side of her handsome cowpoke, lawman.

She handed him her empty, and he stashed it with his in the pack. "We've both suffered loss and survived. I'm finally coming out the other side of a long, dark tunnel." She'd not expressed it quite that way before.

"I understand what you mean. I survived darkness of sorrow quicker because of Cy. I didn't have time to drown in grief. A baby requires a momma. He didn't have the luxury of one for long. So I had to make up for it and be mommy and daddy. Cy needed me in the here-and-now, not lost in misery. Kids realize if you aren't *all in* with them. I didn't want him suffering any more than necessary." He didn't sound bitter in any way, only lucky.

163

"You're a wise, strong man, Leo Sanders. I'm proud knowing you."

He trotted to her side and gazed at her sweetly. "That's good, because I absolutely adore you, Chloe Roberts. Say you'll keep seeing me."

Feeling flames rising in her cheeks, she grew bold. "I couldn't stop if I wanted to." Enough had gone unsaid, and they'd wasted too much time. "One more thing I want cleared up." She eyed him sideways.

Sitting erect, his hands rested holding reins loosely on the saddle horn. He stared her in the eye. "Anything. What do you want to know?"

"Why do you and Tray hate each other? Don't tell me—the murder case. I want to understand the personal side of it." Dread of bringing Tray's name up forced a deep inhale into her lungs. As her chest rose to accommodate it, she hoped she hadn't just ruined what they'd accomplished so far.

"Oh, yeah, fine. I don't mind. Tray was engaged to Claire when I met her and commuting back and forth between New York and Lexington where she lived. After accepting his proposal misgivings set in. Something about him rubbed her wrong. He was demanding, bossy and tried to isolate her from friends and family. She kept putting off setting a date, hoping things would change. Our meeting was the end of their engagement. We knew from the first we had to be together. She broke it off with him, and we married six weeks later. Ackerson resents me and thinks I stole his woman. If Claire had been sure about him, I wouldn't have stood a chance with her."

"Of course, you're right, but I see why he'd hate you. It's easier to blame you than consider it might be him. Why do you hate Tray?" He was confiding in her, and they were discussing serious matters. It was a good sign their bond was slowly healing.

"I ran into Ackerson when he first moved to Sweetwater. He asked about Claire. I told him about her death, and he accused me of being the reason she died. He threatened to get even—whatever that means." He winced. Rippling muscles tightened visibly through the sweaty shirt clinging to his stomach. His eyes filled with moisture. Drawing in a heavy breath, he glanced at the sky, and his hands twitched against the reins. Zorro quivered and turned his head to the side to glimpse his master.

Eyes wide, Chloe frowned. "Why would he blame you? You didn't make her ill."

"We learned of Claire's astrocytoma or glioblastomas too late. The condition is incurable, and the fastest growing and most common tumor in adults. Specialists tried unsuccessfully to halt progress. Surgery wasn't an option. Chemotherapy and radiation made her violently ill. Alternating electrical field therapy helped her grow marginally better, but nothing stopped the bastard cancer from spreading swiftly until she gave out. Damn, I was helpless to stop it and the feeling never left me."

"It's understandable. I'm sorry, Leo. I didn't mean to dredge up traumatic memories. It was a difficult situation, and you did everything possible to save Claire. Where does Tray get off blaming you for her death?" She shook her head. "I'd never have suspected he'd act so callously, until lately." She was seeing new sides of both men.

"Dumb Ass thinks his money could've given her better medical care, and she'd be cured. He doesn't understand. There's no cure. Her illness was discovered too late. We tried every option, but it progressed at lightning speed. She was gone before reality sank in. All the money in the world couldn't save her."

"I'm sorry for your loss. Tray had no right. I'm sure he doesn't understand what happened. He's blaming you out of desperation." She'd felt much the same way losing Hal. Sympathy for both men surged through her, but sorrow didn't excuse Tray's actions.

They rode for a while then returned to the barn and tied the horses to a stall wall. Leo helped Chloe unsaddle Jazz. Together they returned equipment to the tack room. He handed curry combs and brushes to her, and their hands touched, and eyes met. Her heart caught. She stopped breathing momentarily.

Leo's free hand came up, and he caressed her cheek with the back of a bent finger. Then he slipped it beneath her hair, cradling her head in his palm.

Her mouth opened in anticipation, and she inhaled. The scent of aging wood, hay, manure, and horse sweat combined with the man's natural oils into an intoxicating fragrance instantly hooking Chloe. She knew it in her heart; she'd never forget the moment.

His face neared hers as his breath crossed her skin. Leo's lips tasted sweet and savory, soft and warm, and fresh and new. She'd forgotten how marvelous a romantic kiss in a new relationship was. Her free hand slid across his shoulder and up his neck holding him to her. Rising on tiptoes she met his bent frame. His moan sent a thrill pulsating through her heart.

She leaned into him. Her breasts grazed his flat belly causing her nipples to harden into pebbles inside layers of cotton separating them. A joyous tingle swept through her. Her pelvis edged toward the man holding her.

The soft, sweet graze was exploratory at first. With his moan, force increased; and his tongue slipped inside the inviting cavity. She sucked savoring the flavor.

His erection began forming, pushing against his jeans and her tummy. A delightful surge shot through her, acknowledging her effect on him.

Tenderly brushing a curl from her forehead, he pulled away. His gaze was filled with promise. His eyes spoke more than words about his emotions.

Fixated in a trance, the longing to be close to Leo was excruciating. Shared intense desire filled the air around them and they were alone in the haze of desire and had forgotten where they were.

Jazz whinnied and stomped the ground. Zorro joined in the fun. Chloe snickered, bringing a finger to her lips. Leo joined them and shook his head.

He fingered a curl by her ear. "I'd love to explore where this leads, but I promised Mom I'd return by now. She has plans for the afternoon, and I need to spend time with Cy. I've missed the little rascal the last couple days, unable to return home until he's down for the night." He screwed his mouth sideways.

His expression indicated how badly he dreaded pulling away. He obviously wanted Chloe as much as she craved him.

"It's okay. There will be time for us. I understand. Besides, I've got appointments this afternoon." It was a good excuse, but nothing she couldn't cancel.

She freed herself from the embrace and wandered into the breezeway. The horses waited to be brushed, so Chloe got to work. Jazzabelle nodded gratefully as she stroked the tall palomino. "Grooming her is soothing, for me as much as her."

Leo was working on Zorro, and their eyes met over the critters. "I enjoy it too." They worked without words for a while. Then Chloe led Jazz toward her stall.

Leo untied Zorro and grabbed his halter. "Let's turn them in the pasture. Morgan will bring them in later to feed." He led the Zorro through the barn out the back door to a red metal gate.

Chloe and Jazz followed. He unlocked the gate and released Zorro's bridle. He pointed the gelding inside the field and Zorro ran a few feet then bucked with joy. Jazz did a crow hopping dance anxious for freedom and making Chloe high-step to keep her from trotting on her boots. Without hesitation Chloe entered the field and unclipped Jazz from the lead rope. She raced to her buddy, and they joyfully romped across the pasture together.

"They're in love." Leo snickered and strolled toward the tack room with Chloe on his trail.

"It's a beautiful thing." She inhaled a deep whiff of fragrance and savoring it, memorized every second. They returned brushes and combs then hung leads on stall walls.

"Sure enough." He snaked his hand around hers. A spark of heat zipped up her arm to her heart thawing something frozen inside since Hal's disappearance, and sending a twitch to her bottom. She hadn't experienced yearning for a romp in the hay since he disappeared. The aging barn would be a fitting scene for a lovely memory. With her luck, she'd get chiggers on her rump. Good there wasn't time.

Leo helped Chloe into his truck then climbed in beside her. His body radiated against her, welding them together as one where their hips met. He gripped her hand like his life depended on it, and she snuggled close.

Feeling his strong heart beat against her, Chloe's head rested on his shoulder. Her eyes closed. Sensations coursed through her being, allowing thoughts to stall, focusing on the moment. She hadn't been as relaxed with anyone since she was a child. It felt safe and right.

Words were irrelevant. They were comfortable in silence.

At their destination, he shifted into park. His hand rested against her thigh as he faced her. "I'd love nothing more than to take you to bed right now. My lips yearn to kiss every inch of your flesh." His voice grew thick and gravely.

Her intake of breath barely sustained her. His speech made time stand still. She smiled and grazed a thumb across softness of his lower lip.

"Making love to you would be wonderful, but there's no hurry. It's not the time." She leaned into him and kissed him tenderly. He tasted delightful of spearmint and a hint of coffee—her new favorite flavor. "Mmm, nice; now, go. Take care of your son. I've got to clean up and go to work."

She shifted to slide away. He hopped out of the truck and circled around, gripping her waist his hands and branding her skin. He lifted her to the ground and snuggled her close. Her nipples tingled against fabric separating tinder skin. She inhaled, as she leaned against him.

He pulled back, keeping them connected but apart so he could look her in the eye. "Chloe, much as I'd love to linger and explore this, there's something I need to tell you." He paused and bit the side of his lip. "There are shady, at best, dealings between Rizzo and Ackerson. The money trail is leading to surprising places. Rizzo is a dangerous character. Keep away from him, if you can. Promise you'll put distance between you and Ackerson." The warning in his eyes was as sincere as his words.

The request didn't rile her. It merely expressed concern. "No worries. Tray and I started getting chummy too quick. Something feels off with him, and my gut told me to back away. If a business relationship only isn't okay with him, it's his problem." Her belly rested intimately against his firm groin. His erection began forming in earnest again making her chuckled inside.

He eased them apart, brushing a hair from her forehead and smiled. "Good to hear. I realize you need his business, but there's something more at play there. I'm concerned for your safety." His brow furrowed.

"I realize that now. Thanks. I'll keep my eyes open and let you know if I see or hear anything suspicious." She trusted Leo. She hadn't experienced anything nearly as powerful for a man in a long time.

Leo bent to plop a kiss on her lips then one on her nose before releasing her. He touched the tip of her nose with a finger. "Ya 'all have a good afternoon, Chloe. Thanks; today was wonderful."

She could listen to Leo's adorable, sweet, southern twang all day, without caring whether he recited love poetry or the dictionary. She walked the short distance to her door, while h rounded the truck and climbed inside.

"I enjoyed it, too." She waved leaning on the door jamb and basking in sunshine warming her face watching as he backed out and waved. His lovable grin mirrored hers.

It was a good start to a perfect day.

CHAPTER 17

Sitting in Gran's dining room before dinner, Ava sipped a melon ball. "It's sweet of you to remember how much I love Midori, Mom."

Angelica's confused blink testified, Ava was wrong about her recollection. Both women acted embarrassed with Ava coloring more than Angelica. Gran's hand shook visibly holding her sweaty, green-filled cocktail glass.

"Of course I remember, Ava. Are you questioning every memory I dredge up, now we know my fate? Please, promise you won't continually remind me where I'm heading." She sipped the cool drink pursing her lips sternly.

Chloe nervously took a large gulp. The anesthetic power of alcohol helped more than its delightful, refreshing flavor. Would they fight from now to eternity? It was unlike either woman to be cross.

"Gran, go easy on her. Mom didn't mean to upset you. We're devastated by what Doc told us. Whatever comes of it, the three of us face it together." She patted her grandmother's slender hand.

Had she lost weight this week? Gran didn't need that.

"I'm sorry, Ava. Hard to believe—I keep wishing we'd never gone to the doctor. Now I know. I live in constant fear." Worry clouded her usual serene mood.

"Please, don't, Mom. Try to simply live the best life you can. Allow Chloe and me to be here for you. I'll try not to fret so. We'll take care of you. Don't worry." Pain in Ava's heart reflected in her eyes.

"I know you will, my sweet girls." She glanced from her daughter to her granddaughter with what appeared pride and gratitude. "Your dad is as shattered, as I am."

"He—" Ava's eyes widened, and her mouth flew open. She shut it consciously then gulped a large sip of beverage. Rolling her eyes, her gaze met Chloe's, as though seeking help.

Was she starting to hallucinate, seeing the dead?

"I'm sure, wherever Grandpa is, he's watching over you and cares deeply for what you're going through." Chloe squeezed the delicate hand. "He's your guardian angel."

Angelica snickered. "That's a good one. Tony would bust a gut laughing at being called an angel. It's probably the first time ever." She teetered, putting a finely manicured nail to her nose. "Tony is anything but. He's a powerful man, a leader and well-respected. Many fear him, but all respect him. He's a brilliant businessman; a charismatic, enchanting lover; and an engaging friend. Angel? No way. My angel has tarnished wings." She snickered.

Chloe laughed at her grandmother's ramblings. Her mother did the same then gave attention toward Chloe, probably as a ploy to change the subject. "Tell me about your date yesterday, Chloe. Mom, Chloe is dating the darling deputy, Leo Sanders." She patted Angelica's hand and released it.

"Oh, that's delightful, darling." Gran appeared relieved at turning attention away from her.

"It was our first actual date, but yes I want to continue seeing Leo. He's the most interesting man I've met in ages. We went trail riding, and it was a perfect day for it."

"What about the businessman you were dating? Wasn't a Troy fellow romancing you? Are you seeing him too?" Angelica hadn't lost her short-term memory yet, though it became more and more selective.

"Tray, Gran, Tray Ackerson. I'm his realtor. We went on one date, and we had lunch in Lexington. I'm classifying it as a business meal. Yes. He's gorgeous, if you like the Greek god type." She winked evilly at her grandmother. Angelica's eyes twinkled.

"We girls find bad boys fascinating. Don't we? How did your meeting go, dear?" Ava sipped her beverage, acting more relaxed now they'd steered talk out of shaky waters.

"Not well. I don't know what Tray thought I could contribute. I don't understand enough about foundations and structural dynamics to have been a help. The vendor is an expert in the field and provided lots of details. I'm sure Tray knew what they meant, but it went over my head. Our time was cut short when the cops showed up."

"Cops?" Ava's brows shot up.

"Yes, Leo and Jaiden dropped in. Mr. Carnes, whose body I found worked for the company, and they wanted to question the CEO, Anthony Rizzo, and some of his staff. Apparently they either think there's a connection. Or they're ruling out possibilities. Something he did at work could've gotten him killed. Personally, I think either his wife or girlfriend did him in. Those two kooks act nutty enough to join forces and knock the dude off." She laughed but considered it a definite possibility.

"Tony? They think he's involved?" Angelica's head tilted staring at Chloe.

175

"I haven't heard anyone call him that, but Tony's short for Antonio. So, yeah, Tony Rizzo. Why, Gran? Do you know him?"

"Of course I do, darling. He's your grandfather." She bit her lower lip, acting as though she felt guilty divulging a secret.

Ava glared. "Nonsense, Mom. Dad's been dead for years."

"No; he's not. I see him at least a couple times a month. He prefers we keep it on the sly. So don't tell anyone—for our safety. Tony has many dangerous acquaintances; you know." She sipped her drink, talking casually as though discussing the menu.

"What the f—?" Ava's eyes spanned wide.

Chloe had never heard her stately mother use such a word. She whipped her phone out. Pulling up the website for his corporation, she searched for a photo of the CEO. She handed the phone to Angelica. "This is Anthony Rizzo, the man I mentioned. Do you know him?"

Ava leaned to view the screen with her mother. Angelica nodded. "That's my Tony, handsome as ever. This photograph doesn't do him justice. I didn't realize you had business with your grandfather." She studied Chloe as though she was the one dropping a bombshell.

"Mother," Ava's voice stammered. "Are you saying this Tony Rizzo is my father? The father I've thought was dead my whole life?"

"Well, darling, for your safety and mine, we separated when you were a babe because of the fuss happening in Newport. Tony's men dropped dead left and right, or went to jail. Many died of *suspicious* circumstances. Our world was topsy-turvy. Tony believed it best to make a clean break, so no one targeted you or me to get at him. He lives in a dangerous world. We always remained a couple but used discretion. Ava, I told you all this years ago." She studied her daughter's shocked expression with confusion and a wrinkled brow.

"Hell, no, you told me nothing of the sort." Ava's voice cracked and grew louder with each word. She had shifted to the edge of her chair.

Chloe moved closer to Angelica and rubbed her forearm. "Gran, are you sure we're talking about the same man?"

"Yes, dear, the man pictured on your screen is your grandfather, Anthony or Tony Rizzo. He's my husband." She patted Chloe's hand then removed it, turning to her daughter. "Ava, your father never deserted you. Don't get mad. He was there in the background for you through every phase of your life. Tony watched over and cared for you. When you were a kid he never missed a ballgame or a celebration. He attended your wedding; though you believed he was a bartender."

"Dad was alive all these years hiding in plain sight? That's appalling. You're asking me not to be mad. Why on earth didn't you tell me?" Chloe feared Ava would have a stroke, her face reddened so.

"I was sworn to secrecy, my dear. Obviously, my condition has loosened my tongue. I probably wasn't supposed to tell you even now. I'm sorry. Danger is a thing of the past. Tony's a legitimate businessman. He's no longer in control of illegal sin-bartering but still has interest in a gambling consortium. However, it is above board and legal now-a-days. Damn it to blazes. I've slipped up. I hope Tony isn't angry." Her frail hands wrung in her lap. It appeared she might burst into tears anytime.

The oven dinged. Angelica stood, smoothed her designer slacks and waltzed into the kitchen to serve. "Come on, girls. The cordon bleu will not wait."

Hugging her mother they joined Gran in the dining room, Chloe understood Ava's desperation. Hal had worked for the gambling group Gran mentioned.

"It will all be okay, Mom. We'll get to the bottom of this together."

"Damn straight we will. We're heading to Lexington first thing tomorrow. Now, let's enjoy the rest of the evening with Mom, while we have the opportunity."

At dinner Gran talked more about the past. "That cute Jack Kennedy—he was a looker and smooth as silk. He was. I didn't care for his brother, Bobbie. He was all about the *busine*ss."

"Business?" Chloe listened intently, this time trying to get to specifics.

"Yes, they were in politics, you know. We lived in a volatile time with crazy Khrushchev in power in Russia, Castro in Cuba and the Cold War going on. Poor Jack was shot in Texas. I grieved for his family, but we suspected it would happen sooner or later. He kept bucking the system. Your grandpa tried helping him. The Cuban boy, Desi, he was of help too. In the end, I figured the hullabaloo put an end to Jack." Sadness on her face indicated she was telling the truth.

"Wow, Mom, talk about perspective. I'd never considered you up on political issues, even as a young person. You sure don't care for it now-a-days."

"I don't care for it dear—never did. It was the people I enjoyed. What little I know, I overheard at dinner or social events."

"It sounds like you knew Lucy and Desi well." In awe of Gran's experience, Chloe wanted to know more.

"Well, certainly. I assumed there was more to that Latin boy than met the eye. He was a decent musician and charming, but not a great enough actor to warrant his fame. My guess is he got help from powerful people. Lucy was the one with talent and street smarts. I liked her. She was smart letting the bad boy go."

Chloe's head ached like someone had tossed marbles into it and shook it to scramble her brain. Bits and pieces of the puzzle came together. Some were downright terrifying.

What if Gran was wrong? What if Anthony Rizzo was still a crook?

He owned part of the consortium Hal worked for. Had Hal and he known each other? Could he shed light on Hal's disappearance? Did Hal have something on Rizzo? Did he put a hit on her fiancé? Was he murdered? Could it have anything to do with Anthony Rizzo's alleged criminal activities?

Why the hell had Rizzo stayed out of their lives and kept his existence secret all these years? Chloe and Ava had lot to learn. Chloe grew adamant to get to the bottom of it—the sooner the better.

CHAPTER 18

The next day Jaiden and Leo examined the murder board trying to discern next steps. "How did it go yesterday with Chloe? She said you were going trail riding."

The glow in Leo's heart since kissing Chloe flickered to a flame. He'd been high on it all day after leaving her. "It was fun. She's an unusual woman. I enjoy her company. She forgave me and understood."

"I love saying I told you so. Chloe Roberts is a stand up kind of woman."

"Yes and she has good instincts. She was getting a sinister vibe from Ackerson and was leery of Rizzo upon meeting him. She decided to back off of a personal with Ackerson." It almost surprised him how relieved he felt. Coming clean had cleared his mind and freed his heart so he could think straighter.

"That's wise of her. I'll bet hearing she isn't romantically interested in Ackerson tickled the crap out of you." She softly punched his arm.

He pretended to stagger backward. His partner knew him well, might as well tell her. "Yeah, not that he's much competition. I was more worried for her safety than anything."

"Yeah, right. Stick with that story. Let's get to work and talk about where we are on the case."

Leo pointed to the dollar sign drawn on the white board. "The stiff's finances aren't clean. He spent more than he made and the money didn't come from credit, or it would show up on his report. He was getting cash somewhere besides his job. He had to be taking payoffs for something. It wasn't enough to think he was stealing from his job place, and he didn't have access to corporate accounts. The corporation was being swindled, but the take was tons more than the deceased was spending. More like he had one over on someone, and they were paying him to be quite about what he knew."

She propped her butt against Leo's desk. "Yeah, he was milking cash from a source, and apparently they got fed up. It could be related to the firm's theft problem, or could be an entirely different situation. Either way, we need to find out who was embezzling from the company."

"Lexington PD is involved in that, and we've shared what we know about the corporate pilfering. They'll take the lead on it, but we've set up a seamless sharing of data, so anything either of us learns about that will automatically be shared with the other team."

Jaiden pursed her lips and nodded. "Great; that way if anything comes from their investigation into the theft pertaining to our murder case, we'll know instantly about it."

He scratched his head. "Right. Let's see, Harvey wasn't the most careful guy in the world. He stashed dough in plain sight. His wife's attorney discovered what he hadn't blown easily, like anyone digging could."

Jaiden drew a chalk line to his bank account, which was now frozen. "I'll bet she was livid finding out how much dough her old man blew on his bimbo."

"Harvey's wife and girlfriend are volatile, but if one of them killed him, they'd likely have shot him more than once." Leo had worked similar cases in the past, so knew this to be the norm.

Wyatt joined them sitting on Jaiden's desk. "In the heat of anger, a lover will almost always empty a chamber into a victim. Those gals would've scratched his eyes out and each other's too, but I don't see benefit to either of them in knocking him off. I believe Harvey's love life sounds secondary, and less likely to have caused his death." The boss's take sounded right, and his experience and knowledge couldn't be questioned.

Leo nodded drawing a line to the Foundation Corporation. "I agree. We need to get to the source of Harvey's funds. He doesn't strike me as the diabolical, scheming, type. He didn't act smart enough to head up an extortion plot. He was more of a *take advantage of the situation* type. I believe old Harvey got lucky and stumbled onto a pot of gold. He was extorting someone. We have no other financial leads to follow at this time, other than from his workplace. If he knew something worth extorting, it would likely come from his job—but not necessarily. In the meantime, that's the direction we need to follow. So, the question is who was pilfering money from the Foundation Corporation, and did they resort to murder to quiet a snitch?"

Jaiden snickered and shivered visibly. "The crook was either too stupid to live or had balls too big for their britches. What kind of fool swindles from Anthony Rizzo?"

"Anthony Rizzo's mobster background as part of the New York Syndicate in his early years connected him to the Cleveland Syndicate that ran Newport, Kentucky as a mecca for gambling, prostitution and sin. Rizzo was never found guilty of crimes other than tax fraud; but he paid a fortune in back taxes when they proved it was owed. The FBI traced questionable income to him when they shut

183

Newport down during the seventies." Wyatt played with a piece of chalk while studying facts, drawing lines between Rizzo, Ackerson and Carnes.

"Yeah; it appears Rizzo, like the rest of the mob, turned legit after that. He's a smart one, even if he is a retired mobster." Jaiden chewed the side of her lip staring at the line of photographs on the board.

"Gangsters, like tigers, have a hard time hiding their stripes. I believe he's still involved in something shady." Leo tapped the photo of Tony Rizzo. Proof was another story.

"Tray Ackerson's finances aren't clean either. Each time he pays for services his business sends two separate checks. One is large, and the other much smaller. The smaller check goes into the company then splits off into two specific overseas accounts. We're tracking those. At first glance one is connected to Anthony Rizzo. I'm thinking the other belongs to Tray Ackerson. His business with the firm appears to be funding special accounts for some unknown purpose. I'd like to get to the bottom of. it" Jaiden braced with hands on hips.

Leo drew a line between Ackerson and Carnes then pointed to employees they hadn't yet cleared. "Harvey Carnes worked closely with his manager, Coy James, and with Ben Thurman, a mid-level executive in his department. Neither has an alibi. Both have access to finances, supply sources, logistics and could have the ability to steal the money. They show no signs of having excessive cash. If involved, they're hoarding it somewhere. We need to talk more with those two."

"We could bring the lot of them in and get to the bottom of it, but I want a run at Rizzo again first. It might be more efficient talking with James and Thurman at their place of employment." Wyatt grabbed his hat. "Want to go with?" He glanced at Leo.

Leo snatched his hat from his desk. "You bet, boss. Let's do it."

"I'm staying here and working money trails. We'll touch base when you return." She strode to her desk and opened her laptop. "See ya 'all later." Jaiden saluted.

"Good deal." Leo race

CHAPTER 19

Chloe stopped at the coffee shop and ordered a couple brews first thing the next morning. She was heading to Ava's house for their mission. Carl Townsend spotted her waiting and sauntered over then slipped an arm around her shoulders.

"Hey, sweet thang, how's it shaking? I understand you're buying the murder house. Sure it's a good idea? It don't sound safe to me. Your mama is probably freaking out." His accent sounded lurid and sleazy sending a shiver down her back.

She shrugged out of his grasp, glancing around. She knew at least half of the crowd of customer and offered them a timid, closed-mouthed smile.

Damn, the bitch will be hounding me again.

"Listen, Carl, keep a respectful distance. The last thing I need is another round with your wife. You know how chatter gets around."

"Don't worry. Stacy's harmless, but a bit jealous of my old flame. I'll keep her off you, sweetie. I don't mean you no harm. I ain't hitting on ya."

Yeah, right.

"Listen, Carl; if I hurt you when I went off to school, I apologize. We weren't right for each other." The closeness was too much for Chloe, and she gazed longingly at the counter for her order.

"I understand. You were ambitious and had to leave to pursue greater things. Our destinies didn't match. I love it here. I was never inclined to leave this sleepy, little burg. T'wern't me you were leaving. You were following your dream." It sounded hokey coming from Carl.

"I'm glad you understand. Still, you need to keep your hands to yourself. I don't want anyone getting the wrong idea about you and me; so back off."

He back-stepped and put hands up in surrender. "Sorry; didn't realize you were touchy."

"I'm not—well maybe a little. You hearing about my offer is a perfect example of the rumor mill. Stacy jumped to the wrong conclusion previously. I don't want her seeking vengeance for something I didn't do. You know how she is. It's in her nature. Stacy has a tendency toward the dramatic."

"Folks mean well, Chloe. Consider it our way of keeping an eye on and helping fellow neighbors. You're right though. Stacy's kind of volatile. " He snickered, obviously got a kick out of his hot-headed wife's antics.

It takes all kinds.

"Thanks for your concern. I don't need or want your help, Carl Townsend. Far as my offer, I haven't heard an answer. Mom doesn't know and has enough on her plate. I don't want to add to it. Keep your damned mouth shut. You hear?" She poked at his chest as she spoke and tried sounding firm, but wasn't sure it would work in the dumb ass.

He nodded with a serious look. "Loud and clear, listen. I'm trying to be a friend here."

"Maybe so, but you're too cozy, coming in here hugging me. Our relationship is long-dead and in the past. Your wife hates my guts. I don't want to antagonize her. You understand?"

He shrugged nodding with a snicker, appearing proud of his wife's jealously.

A young woman behind the counter called Chloe's name. She retrieved her bag and a paper tray holding two cups.

Carl blocked her exit. "Listen, Chloe, the last thing I want is to cause trouble for you. Old habits are hard to break. Once upon a time touching you was a natural response."

"No, not after all these years; you need to respect me and your wife, and keep your hands to yourself. Thanks for your concern, but I'm capable of handling my life."

"I'm really sorry, Chloe." His face screwed up. His handsome features pinked, and his tone softened. "I didn't mean to intrude or cause you problems. I'm sorry I got too chummy. I apologize for Stacy. She's always been green-eyed where you're concerned. You're beautiful, smart and hve got your life together. She envied you—still does."

"Wow, she sure has the wrong idea about me." Chloe shook her head in awe. "Besides, Stacy's good looking." *In a slutty sort of way.*

"I'm really afraid for you. I wasn't hitting on you— honestly. I love my wife and kids. I feel badly about how we parted when you went to college. You had a scholarship and were destined for grand life in the big city. Going to community college and working the family business was enough for me. I'm happy. I'll make sure Stacy knows I have no romantic interest in you, and you don't want me either. She won't bother you no more. I promise." He actually seemed penitent.

School didn't help his grammar, but his speech sounded sincere. "I'm glad for you. Thanks for worrying about me, but there's no need. I'm good."

"Okay, then. Sorry to keep you." He backed away allowing her to exit.

How could anyone find joy with Stacy Smyth? She could be pretty with less makeup and decent clothing. Carl seemed to find her attractive the way she was.

Maybe she dressed like that for him. Who knows or cares?

Lucky bastard.

It was sweet that Carl cared. Relief washed through her when he'd agreed to keep wacko Stacy off her back. Chloe had enough problems.

With sparse conversation on the trip, Chloe had time to think. She was proud of her mother. Ava was obviously furious and confused, but kept it together with grace, deep in thought. Chloe didn't bother trying to chat. Ava was best left alone now. She had her own worries about their visit.

Finally they arrived at Anthony Rizzo's workplace. They entered the facility on a mission ready to take no prisoners.

Rizzo's assistant smiled recognizing Chloe. "Good morning Ms. Roberts. I'm surprised to see you. You don't have an appointment with Mr. Rizzo today. Do you?" She confusedly glanced over her computer screen at his schedule.

"No, Katy, we don't; but he'll see us anyway." The liar mobster wasn't about to keep them out. Without slowing her pace, Chloe charged to the door and snatched the knob.

Katy hopped from her desk rushing toward them like an avalanche. Not successful in stalling their entrance, she stepped into the surprised man's office behind them.

"Mr.—" Katy's apologetic expression almost made Chloe sorry; but one couldn't argue need for a dramatic entrance. She hoped surprising Rizzo helped lessen power of her confidant grandfather.

"It's okay, Katy. I'll see the ladies." Surprise on his face was quickly replaced with a congenial smile as he stood. "Come in and make yourselves comfortable." His arm waved toward luxurious guest chairs facing his desk.

Ava strode in like a warrior prepared for battle. She was on a quest, and there was no stopping her. Anger bloomed in all its glory on her regal face.

Ava's feisty mother was married to the mob. Her long-dead father was alive. Her stony expression communicated, she would get the straight story, or hell would pay.

Once they were seated, he plopped into his desk chair. "Welcome, ladies. I'm not sure what spurred it but it's time we had this encounter. The wonder is we haven't stumbled over each other long before now." He remained graceful, courteous wearing a take-charge expression.

"It was your doing—you controlled everything. Your decree forced us into lives of complete fabrications. Who are you to make such a decision?" Ava shot the words without a quiver in her heated voice. Her shoulders held firm; and she sat erect, hands folded in her lap.

"I'm your father, Ava, and your grandfather, Chloe. It is so good to finally admit it. I've loved and watched over you your whole lives, keeping you safe from a distance." Warmth and affection beamed from his dark eyes.

Chloe's gaze spanned the room. A credenza surface lined with framed photos of Ava at her wedding, graduation and one in a basketball uniform. Two players she was hugging after a victory looked like young versions of Wyatt and Justin. Shots of Chloe as a baby, a toddler, Home Coming Queen in her senior high school year and at college graduation scattered across a wall behind his desk. Photos had been removed for her benefit when Chloe had met Rizzo with Tray.

Did Tray know?

"Did you take those pictures?" Chloe barely recognized her voice. Anger persisted, but was rapidly softening. Rizzo's attitude made her decide to hear his side of the story before jumping to conclusions.

A proud smile graced his face. "Mostly. Some were gifts from Angel. I never missed a game you played, Ava, or any significant event in your life. I was there . . . in the background—a stranger. I was at the hospital for your birth, Chloe." Something like love flowed thickly in his voice and filtered his eyes causing them to go milky with moisture.

"How dare you? Why didn't you let me know you were alive? I mourned you every day. It's not fair." Fury in Ava's voice was like none Chloe had heard before from her proper mother. It began to wane to sound more like remorse.

"I understand your anger, and you have every right to it. I waived the option of forgiveness when I let you go, but I've loved and wanted you always. You need to know giving you up was the hardest thing I've done—and I've done awful things. I'm not a man you'd proudly call father. When you were small it was a lawless time. I was at the hilt of dreadful business ventures. Many enemies would gladly harm you and Angel to get at me. The solution to your safety was to hide your connection to me."

"Mother kept your secret. Being separated from you must've hurt her. I know it did me. I grieved for you and missed having a dad." Her stormy face was slathered with a liberal amount of disgust.

"Your mother understood. She was with me in the middle of the worst time and recognized as I, what peril you were in. She agreed to the arrangement. In fact, she concocted the idea. It was brilliant and worked. She's made a valiant effort to raise you well. We've stayed close, discreetly seeing each other leading a freestyle marriage and have remained faithful. I ensured your mother and you were well cared for. She never had to scrimp or do without and had the best of everything."

The magnitude of the situation was sheer madness, and Chloe's head spun. The horse had left the stable, so they had to lasso it one way or another. She yearned to shift focus and help Ava accept the state of affairs so they could determine a way forward.

"I can't be angry with Mother. She's ill and needs me—needs all of us. Don't try and blame her." Ava shot him a defiant glare.

"I take full responsibility and would never blame your mother. I waived the right to forgiveness when we separated, unaware how much agony of not being in your life would cause all of us."

"So—it's *all* about you." Ava scowled down her nose.

"Heaven's no. It's about your, Chloe's and Angel's safety." He proved no easy conquest. "I can weather any storm. You, however, needed sanctuary."

"Did you bankroll my business as my silent investor?" Exasperation ruled her tone, and she acted as though she'd begun to understand how dire the problem had been. Stress was difficult for Ava. She normally avoided drama. Chloe was amazed how well she was handling this.

He nodded, allowing his love to shine so sincerely it appeared coming from his soul. Maybe he wasn't such a horrible person. "Yes. I've treasured you every day, and Angel is the love of my life. We're not a classic-style clan—and certainly won't become a traditional family now. I'd like to participate in your lives, if you'll have me. Granted I'm not much to take pride in. I have a legacy of dirty business. That's in the past. I've worked hard over the years changing and growing legitimate companies. I've turned things around; trying to build something you wouldn't be ashamed of." His arms spanned out as though displaying some visual.

Ava's head spun away hiding tears and trying to hold them in. Tony was pushing boundaries she'd set in her mind.

Chloe's heart ached, wishing she could make it easier. She stroked her mother's arm, soliciting a close-mouthed smile from the woman staring at carpeting between her feet.

The threesome had one thing in common. They loved Gran and needed to consider her needs.

"Gran is ill. Tests show she has early-onset dementia due to Alzheimer's. She's forgetful, but knows what's going on most of the time. She's starting to lose short-term memory, while long-term recollection is currently stable. Deterioration will continue, and she will forget events then people. Eventually she won't know us or who she is and won't remain capable of living alone forever. She'll begin to forget things like turning the stove off or where she is and will become a hazard to herself. She won't recall to take medication or if she took it, if she ate or know how to fix food for herself. Hopefully it will be a long time before she becomes an invalid. She will require continual nursing until her heart eventually forgets to beat. Until then, we have a tough battle. We must band together to care for her." The more she talked, the harder tears fell. Chloe sobbed like a baby by the time she finished speaking. Thinking of Angelica's worsening and finally passing on filled her with a sense of deep sadness. She couldn't imagine a world without her spicy grandma, but someone had to explain it to the man.

"I figured it was happening, and she tried explaining what the doctor said. I'm concerned; and totally agree, Chloe. Thank you for spelling it out. I'd never desert

Angel. We're in this together for better or worse. I want and treasure every second I can spend with her. Let me suggest we keep things normal as we can for as long as possible. I won't commit Angel to a home, but will ensure she has the finest care. In a few months or weeks, whenever she needs it, we'll hire a companion to live with her. Eventually we can bring on a full-time nursing staff. We must spend time with her and focus on making happy memories while her mind is with us. I dread the day she's merely here in body. I'm not sure how I'll survive without my Angel. She's my rock." As he spoke, his dark eyes filled with moisture. His voice was tender and loving, and he didn't bother wiping tears drizzling down his ruddy cheeks.

"Thank you Mr. Rizzo . . . Tony—. Blast it, I don't have a clue what to call you." Chloe bit her lower lip.

He leaned forward clasping hands on the desktop. "Call me whatever you wish, Chloe; but know, I'm here for my Angel in her time of crisis. She was there for me through some extremely ugly stuff. I'm in it for the duration. Count on me footing the bill for whatever she requires. It's my woman we're talking about. She's my everything." He sniffed and pulled out a white handkerchief from his suit jacket.

Chloe found new respect for the handsome, Italian-descent gentleman. He appeared to value his word and was in touch with his feelings, not afraid to express sentiment. She didn't know him well yet, but could tell she could depend on him. She leaned forward trusting he wouldn't lie. "Mr. Rizzo."

"Hopefully someday you'll call me Grandpa, or some form of it. If you don't want to yet, Tony will work."

"Okay, Tony." She cleared her throat. The name didn't roll naturally over her tongue. With time and luck she'd get used to it—if Mom was open to building a relationship with him. Chloe wasn't about to hurt her mom. Ava had been hurt too much already.

Having a grandfather was an appealing notion. Dad's disinterest since marrying a chick almost her age and starting a new and improved family had pushed Chloe to the bottom of his priority list.

Buzzing in her head warned, and she gulped in air for strength. It might be too soon to count the chickens "I understand you're part of The Triple Play Consortium. You've actively stalked us all my life, so I assume you realize my fiancé, Hal Spence, worked for you in New York; and that he disappeared without a trace. What can you tell me about it?" Her heart prayed his answer would either set her free or shed no new light whatsoever. It depended on whether he had instigated or had involvement in the disappearance.

His face grew serious, and he winced. Their eyes locked. "First, let me tell you how sorry I am for your loss. It's awful, what you've gone through."

She blinked back tears Hal's disappearance continued to bring. "Thank you, Tony," she murmured.

He pursed his lips keeping her gaze steady and spoke assuredly with confidence. "I am a third owner of the consortium formed by me and a couple of partners to support our gambling establishments in Las Vegas. When gaming expanded legally across the States, we've grown with it legal and above board. I didn't realize your Hal worked there, until he was reported missing and the police came to visit me during the investigation. I know absolutely nothing about what happened to him. Understanding what he meant to you, I tried to get to the bottom of it by hiring a team of investigators. I've researched, done inquiries and found nothing. I don't suspect his employment had anything to do with the vanishing. Chloe, please believe me. I wouldn't do anything to intentionally cause your pain." He winced. His eyes appeared sincere, and his tone sounded earnest.

"I appreciate your honesty. I'm not accusing you, but had to ask. The connection is too strong to ignore." She believed him. Relief eased tension in her neck and shoulders she hadn't realized lived there.

"What do we do now?" Ava eyed him through glazed eyes. She'd had enough for one day.

Chloe felt protective of her, but was exhausted as well. Tony Rizzo clearly meant her no harm. He wanted the best life possible for her mother.

"We figure out how to include Tony in our lives." She held her mother's quivering hand. "Your dad is alive, Mom. He loves and wants you. It is a joyous thing. I wish Dad felt for me the way Tony cares you."

Ava frowned, and her lips quivered. She brushed a curly lock off Chloe's forehead with a manicured finger. "I'm sorry, my girl. Your dad will regret ignoring you someday—his loss, sweetheart, more than yours. You have Tony." She glanced at her father with a willful smile, meeting one of his. He nodded. "He's here for you, too."

Ava spun in her seat, as the woman-in-charge Chloe was used to seeing took over. "Dad, dinner is at seven at Mom's place every Thursday. Don't miss it." She smiled sweetly speaking like the invitation was no big deal.

Any veneer remaining melted from his expression. "I wouldn't miss it for the world. Your mother is a world-class chef. I'll ask her to make lasagna." His shoulders rocked back, and his chin rose humbly.

Ava chuckled. "We recently learned the origin of Mom's lasagna recipe."

He chortled and reached a hand to pat hers resting there. Ava's head jerked to meet his eyes, but she didn't pull her hand away.

He grinned with pride. "Angel has a way with people, especially men. She can wheedle anything she wants from a gentleman. My gutsy girl had old Frankie begging to share his family recipe with her."

Chloe sniggered, and as part of the tension in the room lifted, it became easier to breath. "I can imagine how it went. Gran is certainly a spirited character."

"Yes, and I see a lot of her in you, Chloe." He nodded with one brow cocked and lips pursed. "She's passed her strong qualities to the two of you. Ava, you got your business acumen from me and your good looks from your mom. You're a powerful entrepreneur. I'm busting with pride in your accomplishments."

Ava's shoulders rolled back, and her chin shot up. "Thank you, Dad. I'll take it as a compliment." She stood. "We should go. We have work to attend to. It's been enlightening. I appreciate your candor and support." She stretched a hand for a shake.

He rounded the table and placed himself between them, sliding an arm round each woman's shoulders; and they stepped toward the door. Chloe felt warm and sheltered beneath his massive limb.

"I'm thrilled you gals came. I understand this visit wasn't easy to initiate. I've wanted to make this talk happen for ages, but there was never a good time."

"There's no such thing." Ava grimaced with a half-smile. "I'm happy. I dreaded what outcome of confrontation might be. It's going to be okay. I'm overwhelmed and thrilled you're alive, and we want you in our lives." She glanced at Chloe, getting a return nod and smile. "See you Thursday, Dad." Ava wiped a tear with the back of her hand looking exhausted. She'd had enough strong emotions for one day but managed a brilliant smile.

"I'm going to like saying it—Dad." She hadn't smiled like that since Chloe graduated from business school.

Things were looking up.

.

CHAPTER 20

Katy hovered at her desk with desperation shadowing her congenial temper, in deep conversation with Leo and Wyatt. Her glance at Tony looked hopeful as his door opened and he exited his lair. His unexpected guests walked, nestled beneath his arms. Tony kissed Chloe's cheek then Ava's before releasing them.

Puzzled looks on Wyatt's and Leo's faces almost made Chloe laugh. She was the one with explaining to do this time.

Tony trod toward the threesome purposefully. "Sheriff Gordon and Deputy Sanders, how may I help you?" He shook hands with the lawmen.

Leo glanced at Chloe with a *what gives* expression. His brows rose, and eyes widened.

She shrugged. Explanation would have to wait.

"Mr. Rizzo, thank you for generously sharing your books with us. It's been a tremendous help. We've uncovered anomalies in your accounting system needing clarification. Inconsistencies may relate to the murder of your employee, Harvey Carnes. We need to question a couple of your employees, and we'd like you to join. Can you meet us at the Sweetwater jail after we take them in?" Wyatt stood with thumbs in his utility belt.

"Certainly." Wyatt's head rocked up and down in answer. Tony glanced at his assistant. "Katy, clear the rest of my day."

To Wyatt and Leo, he nodded. "No problem, officers. I'll see my family out and drive to Sweetwater. I have one stop to make. I'll get to the precinct in a couple hours."

Leo's mouth flew open looking confused. Wyatt smiled with crinkled brows, obviously as confused as Leo. "Perfect. Thank you for accommodating us."

Tony glanced at Ava and Chloe. "I need to stop by Angel's. She's expecting me."

Wyatt and Leo stepped out of the reception area heading toward an elevator bank.

Chloe tiptoed and kissed her grandfather's cheek. She made a conscious decision to welcome him in her life and to trust the ruthless man. "Bye, Tony. See you Thursday."

Ava squeezed the hand Tony offered, then leaned over and pecked his cheek. "I'm glad you're okay, Dad. See you at Mom's Thursday."

"I can hardly wait." Tony patted Ava's shoulder tentatively. This time she didn't flinch.

Elevator doors opened and the two fellas who had attended Tray's meeting with Tony stepped off. Wyatt and Leo stood nearby waiting for a down elevator. The characters glanced around suspiciously and visibly jerked sideways seeing Wyatt and Leo readying to board. Leo recognized them and whirled around to stop them from back-stepping into the closing elevator doors. They shifted sideways avoiding Leo's grasp and gaped the space as though looking for a way out.

"Coy James, hold up. We're here to see you and Ben Thurman." Leo's voice was severe and demanding, as he moved quickly in the direction of the frantic men.

Coy James stopped with a haunted expression on his face; Ben Thurman high-tailed it out of the lobby. Chloe and Ava watched mesmerized, as events happened so fast, she hardly knew what hit her.

Ben Thurman, resembling a possum caught in headlights, shot out of the Men's room near where the women huddled.

The air chilled. Not a breath was heard.

Wyatt was across the room cuffing his boss, Coy James. Ben's eyes flashed wildly, and he jerked sideways, jumping behind Chloe. He shoved Ava away, and she stumbled and fell a short distance away. She slithered to the wall and hid behind a potted plant.

Ben grabbed Chloe's arm and wrenched it tight and high behind her back. Buzzing in her head blocked whispers from across the room. She recoiled and struggled silently telling herself to breathe. Searing pain in her shoulder and arm caused her to go limp. Thurman yanked her up and against his frame, slipping a hand around her neck and almost cutting off her air. He shoved an automatic pistol to her head, and cold steel chilled her temple.

Prattled, heavy, erratic breath emanated fear. He smelled of sweat. A chill shot through her, and she shivered. The man was clearly unstable and capable of harming her. Images of the bloody corpse she'd discovered flashed through her mind, and she shuddered.

"I'm backing out of here and taking this bitch with me." Ben's words quivered, but meaning was clear and convincing. She was his leverage.

Across the room Wyatt shoved Coy to the floor and firmly pointed. Coy cowered against the wall quaking and terrified.

Wyatt held his hands up in surrender taking a step toward them. Tony was nowhere to be seen, but his office door stood open.

Pzzt The sound came from Katy's cubical.

Ben's focus was on Wyatt as he edged toward them. Leo slipped inside the opened door and disappeared.

Wyatt halted with each step, articulating his position to her kidnapper. He was easing with baby steps toward them. "I can't let you take her. There's no way you're leaving this building with Ms. Roberts. You're in over your head, buddy. Turn her loose. We'll forget this happened. You've got enough trouble on your plate, Thurman."

Wyatt's tone and swagger came across calm and collected. Chloe knew him well enough to realize, inside he was anything but. He was a pro and the best man to have on her side in a perilous situation.

Ava looked desperate with mouth open and eyes wide. Chloe needed to come out of this unscathed. Her resolve grew because Ava couldn't handle losing her. It bolstered her strength as she drew a steady, slow breath, and every nerve stood on edge. Even her hair felt alive.

Wyatt eased forward with his hands in the air. "Wait a minute, Thurman. Don't do this. Don't hurt the woman. You and Mr. James need to come to the station for questioning. That's all we want. Whatever you've done, you don't want to add kidnapping to it. Turn Ms. Roberts loose." Even though he wasn't, Wyatt managed to sound in control.

Ben edged backward dragging her toward the front stairwell. She tried resisting, making him force her along; but he held her firmly against him forcing her steps.

Peripheral vision showed a familiar frame advancing along a narrow corridor to her left. Leo rushed toward them silently, with his weapon trained on Ben.

Now or never.

Chloe spun around to face Ben. Her movement jarred his grip, and he released her neck. She head-butted the short man with as much power as she could muster.

The gun went off.

Her knees gave way, and she sunk to the floor. Her head ached like an SOB, and stars floated across fluttering eyelids. She felt Ben's body moving downward as though falling with her.

Had Leo been shot?

Leo bombarded the dazed man knocking the pistol from his grasp. It hit the floor and spun round and round, finally landing near Ava. She recoiled and froze.

Ben had plopped heavily on top of Chloe. In a stupor, she struggled to shove him off her. Leo jerked the blob, and his weight shifted away.

Wyatt sped over and snatched a plastic bag from his pocket. He picked the gun up with it then sealed the bag. Wyatt returned to his prisoner, yanked James to his feet and shoved him toward the elevator.

Leo had her assailant cuffed by then and pushed Ben Thurman toward the sheriff. Wyatt ushered the prisoners out of the office building.

Leo drew Chloe from the floor into his arms, lifting and settling between his two.

Her throbbing head rested on his shoulder, and she allowed tears to flow. Her body trembled out of control, and she occasionally sniffed, struggling to breath. She inhaled intoxicating scent of the man she craved. She'd never felt as secure, enveloped in Leo's long, strong arms with him towering over her. Her breasts pillowed against his firm, rippling belly.

"I feel like a horse kicked my skull," she whimpered into his chest.

Tony clambered from his office thrusting a revolver into his belt. Katy followed him with her hands over her mouth and wide eyes. Tony helped Ava scramble from the floor then enveloped her in his arms. Ava melded into them until finally her quaking ended, and they stepped to where Leo cradled Chloe.

"Thanks, Mr. Rizzo. Sending me through your office down a side hallway worked perfectly. So did your granddaughter's quick thinking." Leo smiled down at her upturned face. His lips grazed her forehead.

Chloe rubbed her hammering temples. "I'm not so sure I did the right thing." They all laughed, and tension began to drift away. Finished bawling like a baby, Chloe tilted and smiled into Leo's beaming eyes. "Thank you, Leo; I could tell you were up to something when you disappeared into Tony's office. No way was the asshole dragging me along as hostage. I was doing something one way or another, and when I heard rustling down the aisle, I figured you were coming to my rescue, and it was perfect timing. Another second and he'd have dragged me into the stairwell. You're officially my hero."

"Woman, you're a tiny piece of heaven with the spirit of a warrior." He bent taking her lips in a kiss she wished would never end. Barely discerning chatter around them as they lingered delightfully, Leo finally pulled away with a dazzling, boyish grin. He turned to those watching with amusement on their faces and shook Tony's hand.

"Nice work, deputy. I'm glad you're quick on your feet. My family is in good hands." Tony winked at Chloe.

"You're welcome, Sir."

"Leo, thank God you were here. I'll never be able to repay you for saving my daughter," Ava gushed.

"I would have it no other way, and no need to thank me. It terrified me when that thug grabbed Chloe." He squeezed Chloe tightly beneath his arm, winked at her then accepted Ava's hug before walking the ladies to Chloe's car.

Wyatt had loaded the prisoners in the cruiser. Leo bent and gave Chloe one last peck through the open driver's side window. "See you later."

"Definitely." She could hardly wait.

Ben Thurman and Coy James were argumentative, as they were cuffed and read their rights when they arrived at the Sweetwater jail. Jaiden deposited Coy in a cube with blank walls, bright lighting, a mirrored wall, and a table with three chairs. She locked his cuffs to a chain attached to the steel tabletop.

Leo parked Ben in an interrogation room down the hall. "Ben Thurman, I understand you're the Head of Purchasing and Construction Coordination at the Foundation Corporation." The sleazy guy nodded with pursed lips. "Your buddy, Coy James, is Harvey Carnes' direct manager. Right?" Again a disgruntled nod. "You're definitely going to jail for the stunt you pulled at the office. The question is, should the charge include murder one or not. Think about that, and we'll be with you when we have time." He shut the locked door and snickered when the suspect cringed.

Wyatt met them outside the doors. "We will play them against each other to get to the truth." Wyatt kicked the heat to eighty-five in the enclosed cubicles. "Let them sit a good length of time until they boil with worry. The worse they feel when questioned, the better." They went to a cubical between the two questioning rooms. It had windows on both sides so they could observe the men waiting to face consequences of their actions. When they were finally sweating, taking long gasps of air and shifting uncomfortably in the hard seats, it was time.

Leo led the process. Wyatt observed from behind the mirrored wall. Jaiden entered with Leo and leaned against a wall checking her nails and looking bored.

Leo sat silently watching Ben for a full five minutes with no expression on his face, letting the suspect stew. His measured, cool voice flowed off his tongue smooth as a shot of Kentucky bourbon.

"So, Thurman, you stole from your employer. You attacked and attempted to kidnap Chloe Roberts in front of two officers of the law and several witnesses. You royally screwed up. You don't appear the stupid type; but looks can be deceptive."

"I have no idea what you think. If you believe I've done something illegal, you're dead wrong." Ben tried looking confused but failed miserably. Nerves got the best of him, and his hand shook as he swiped beads of sweat from his forehead. "I saw you there and thought something awful was going on. I just wanted to get the heck out of there."

"So you attempted to kidnap Ms. Roberts and drag her to safety. Right. Nice try. We're not buying it. Let's see now. We've got attempted kidnapping and assault with a deadly weapon." Leo counted off on his fingers. "By the way, we're testing your pistol for the murder weapon. We have you red-handed for theft. The money trail is clear from you to an off-shore account. Where did you get the idea—from the setup of the owner's retirement funds?" Leo splayed his hands on the stainless tabletop.

"You've got nothing on me." Ben glared, gripping his hands together attempting to stop quivering.

"By the way, the woman you attacked is the granddaughter of your company CEO. That's two strikes against you with Mr. Rizzo. Guess you were clueless. Anthony Rizzo is an ex-mobster with a sinister past. If the law doesn't get you, the mob probably will. Come to think of it, they likely have connections in the pen, too. We could turn you lose now, and let them save tax payers a lot of dough." Leo chuckled.

Ben blanched to ghostly white. Confusion showed on his face, but he was wise enough to hold his curiosity.

"We've got you both clearly marked for embezzlement. Evidence shows you've milked dough off construction bills for years. Rizzo isn't happy with you—if you know what I mean. Damn, son. You're dumber than I thought. Speaking of dead," he paused a couple of beats. "You or your buddy Coy James, are responsible for Harvey Carnes' murder. The question is which one of you is guilty." Leo allowed his long, slow cackle to reverberate so it would do the trick. Ben visibly shook, and his breathing grew erratic, clearly surprised by the news about his employer.

"You can't prove anything." Ben glared belligerently. His pallid complexion attested he got the point.

"I can, and will. You blazed a clumsy money trail and are stupid enough to steal from one of the most notorious mobsters in the country." What little blood remained drained from Ben's face. Leo snickered loudly making no secret Ben's predicament tickled him. "You didn't know? Hilarious." Leo shook his head and rolled his eyes.

Jaiden shifted from leaning on one leg to the other with a heavy sigh and checked her watch, continuing to act bored, as though the interrogation was a formality. "Rizzo's legit now, but people who rub him wrong usually disappear."

"Rizzo?" The name flowed slowly across Ben's tongue. "Oh shit." He clutched his hands together on the table to stall their quivering.

"Here's the deal, Thurman. One of you two dudes did Carnes in. Fess up first, and we'll work with the system to help lighten your sentence. Don't and your buddy gets the deal. Last one to talk gets shit." Leo nodded Jaiden's way. She stood erect, and together they strolled toward the door.

She turned to the man chained to the desk. "Dude, I recommend you work with us on this. Word has it, Rizzo likes torturing victims before killing 'em." She winked then shut the door quietly behind them.

They entered the dark room next door, where Wyatt watched.

"What do you think?" Leo eyed his boss.

"Thurman's scared. He'll talk, the question is how much. He's definitely guilty of the theft, but I don't believe he's the brains behind the operation. He doesn't strike me as a leader or strategic planner, and he fumbled the hostage thing. Let's see how it goes with the other perp."

"He'll give us whatever he's got on the sting. I feel it in my bones; but if he was the shooter, he may not own up to it. If he didn't do Carnes, he'll definitely squeal on whoever did—if he knows." Through the glass Ben Thurman fumbled with his hands and wiped sweat from his brow.

They turned to view Coy James brewing in the other cubbyhole-sized space. He twisted in his seat and repeatedly swiped moisture from his face. Wyatt liked his suspects hot and irate.

Wyatt sauntered in and nodded. He sat on a chair against the wall and leaned forward. Clasping his hands with elbows on knees, he stared at the floor.

Leo meandered into the room and took the chair beside Wyatt. They quietly watched their captive, allowing silence to inspire fear.

Leo recognized Coy's fake calmness as he rustled in his seat. Lack of luster in his gaze gave him away. So did a tremble in his hands before he folded them on the table. An imitation smug grin curved his thin lips.

Sensing his prey's angst, Leo took charge with an intense stare. "James, we brought you here today to issue an arrest. The question is for what exactly. You had quite an enterprise going—until someone got careless and stupid."

He grimaced stiffly. "What the hell do ya think you have on me? I've done nothing to warrant being hauled to this hillbilly berg and held like a criminal. I want answers—now. Arrest me, or turn me loose." He pounded a chained hand, and handcuffs clanged against metal.

Wyatt snickered. "Demand all you want. It'll get you nowhere. We've got you sitting on a pile of cash you ripped off. You're going to the pokey for embezzlement. The question is, are we adding murder one to the sentence."

Pausing well-rehearsed monologue, Leo allowed the glazed face on James to freeze as information gelled. "Here's the deal. You and Ben Thurman stole from the Foundation Corporation. That's a given. Which of you assholes murdered Harvey Carnes? We've explained the deal to your buddy in the next room. You have the same deal. Ben's had time to mull it over and should be ready to spill his guts. One of you killed Mr. Carnes. Whichever of you gives what we need to solve the crime will garner leniency. The other gets the book thrown at him. Give it up, Coy. Did you shoot Harvey, or did your pal do it?" Leo spoke slowly, with a matter-of-fact manner and without his gaze wavering. His eyes stayed locked on his victim.

James winced visibly then blinked several times. His chest rose and fell drawing big gulps of air. His self-importance had waned, and his shifty eyes began to glass over. "I have no idea what you're talking about. The crazy bitch Carnes was married to *knocked him off*. Or the slut he was sleeping with did him in. You're barking up the wrong tree." He appeared ready to cry.

Leo laid a file in front of him and flipped through several pages to select a document showing Coy's identification number on an off-shore account. He pointed to the slip of paper he'd discovered in Coy James' desk. "This has been checked by a handwriting analysis expert. You wrote this note with your account number, password and amount of the latest deposit on it. We've checked the account and know the amount you've accumulated. It would be impressive, if I didn't know its origin." He pulled another sheet from the folder.

James' head spun sideways and he blinked several times. A loud gush of wind slipped through his lips. "That ain't mine. It must've been planted. What do you mean?"

"No need denying it's yours. We've got you and Thurman. Why'd you kill Harvey Carnes? We found Harvey's stash of cash, but it isn't as much as the two of you have accumulated. Was Carnes in on your scam? Did he double cross or rip you off? Or was it blackmail?"

"You're bluffing. I didn't kill no body. You need to turn me lose." He sounded pitiful with his last ditch effort, but his words held no power.

"I could do that, but your boss wouldn't be as forgiving. You know who you swindled, you asshole? Tony Rizzo is a mobster kingpin. What kind of fuck up rips off the mob?" Wyatt laughed a slow, easy chuckle. Coy blanch as white as the spots on Wyatt's new pinto colt.

Leo stood. Wyatt leaned on his elbows expressionless. "Mr. James, you're going away for a long time. We're going after the death penalty for you." A large exhale gushed from their target, as they strode from the room.

Before Leo shut the door behind them, he calmly turned. "Coy, you've got five minutes—maybe less if your buddy is ready to talk. If you decide to level with us, knock on the table. Otherwise, we'll meet again with Ben Thurman and let you know how it went."

The door snapped closed before Coy James could speak. They waited outside to see if he knocked. Nothing but moaning filtered through the door, so they retired to the observation area to watch Coy and Ben through mirrors.

Wyatt glanced from one to the other. "It's a tossup which will confess first."

Jaiden observed both men from her chair and snickered. "You played them perfectly. I'd say five minutes. Then drag their asses past the bullpen, and let them get a load of their boss. We'll go at them again after the lineup. The others are ready."

Wyatt nodded, and they all headed into the bullpen to set things up.

❤❤❤❤

Wyatt cordially greeted and chatted with Anthony Rizzo leading him to his office. He propped the door open so the suspects would get an unobstructed gape at him. Wyatt fixed two cups of coffee then pulled files from his desk, ignoring them in lieu of building rapport with his guest.

"Thanks for coming in today, Mr. Rizzo. Sanders told me we interrupted a meeting with the Roberts women. We didn't mean to screw up a real estate deal you're working on. So if you need me to talk with Ava or Chloe to clear any misunderstanding up, let me know. I'll happily take care of it. We don't want you to suffer repercussions from the way we played the scene." Wyatt leaned back casually in his chair.

Rizzo eased further into his seat, and his hands flashed up. His side faced the wall of windows and open door leading to the bullpen. "No problem. It wasn't a business meeting, and we were finished."

"Oh, do you know Ava and Chloe personally? I wasn't aware you had more than a professional link with Chloe through Tray Ackerson."

"Actually, her connection with my company through Tray is professional. He's a partner in my firm, but he

213

leaves the day-to-day to me. Ava is my daughter; and Chloe my granddaughter."

Wyatt had ushered the prisoners to the cruiser immediately after their capture and was more than curious. Hullabaloo in the station and prisoners in the backseat of their vehicle, he and Leo hadn't found time to talk much.

Allowing his shock to register on his face, Wyatt shook his head. "Wow, I had no idea. The Roberts women aren't guarded with their personal lives, but they kept their relationship with you close to the vest." Surprisingly Ava hadn't said a word, though they'd been close friends since grade school.

"I'm a private person. I'm sure you understand." Rizzo seemed to measure his words.

"Certainly, no sweat; anyway, we wanted you here because there's something going on inside your firm you may not be aware of. We uncovered several ties between off-shore accounts and your company. We haven't identified owners of two of them, but we believe one belongs to Tray Ackerson." Hesitating, he studied Rizzo's expressionless face.

"It's easily explained. Tray and I built the Foundation Corporation together. Our contracts specifying retirement funds be deposited into our off-shore accounts. Tray also gets a kick-back—perfectly legal—for any business his other companies throw our way. It comes to him in the form of a deposit of ten percent of his total invoice. That goes into his retirement fund."

"I noticed the anomaly each time Mr. Ackerson pays an invoice. Would you mind allowing us to review those contracts?"

"I would mind, but rest assured, our team of attorneys ensured they are legitimate. We devised the two-charge program to simplify the process for the accounting team. They receive both payments then fund his account with the lower amount."

It made sense. "Thank you. That explains two of the four accounts we uncovered. Do you mind explaining why you and Mr. Ackerson decided to house your retirement funds outside the U. S.?"

"I do mind, and don't believe it's pertinent." He didn't flinch as he spoke.

Wyatt didn't have probable cause to push either request, and the man had been extremely helpful so far. He needed him for one additional thing, so didn't want to rile him too much.

"Very well. The remaining two trails have been linked to your employees, Coy James and Ben Thurman and have been funded with cash they stole from your company. The murder victim worked with these two. Harvey was spending remarkably above his income level, and we found a significant bundle of dough in his possession. We believe he was in cahoots with James and Thurman in some way." Was that anger boiling in his companion's eyes? "The bulk was split between Thurman and James. We don't believe Carnes was involved in embezzling, though he might have known about it. Your financial records prove Ben and Coy bilked monies skimming from each project, supplying inferior equipment and materials, and sometimes short-changing jobs by delivering less than ordered. We aren't sure which one is the *brains of the operation*, but they're both involved."

"The guy was put down because of this theft." Rizzo's statement was more than a question. He appeared thinking heavily, as he glanced down.

Wyatt gave him a moment for it to set in and wished he could hear thoughts skimming through Rizzo's mind. The man was a master at controlling emotions and action, but he was clearly pissed. Finally Tony met his eyes.

"Carnes' connection?" Again his words were dignified and not rushed.

"Questionable. His cache was a drop in the bucket compared to what the other two pulled in. Carnes was either a junior partner in larceny, or he knew and was paid for his silence. Not sure yet what got him killed, but we're confidant one of those two did him in. Neither man has an alibi. Both had something to gain with Carnes out of the picture."

Watching the regal gentleman visibly fume was almost comical. Rizzo was livid and let it show. He was capable of ridding the world of two bumbling crooks easily, but it was not his way in today's world.

"I need your help. You must realize your reputation precedes you. I'd like to use your past to our advantage, if you don't mind. Considering these punks stole from you, I'm betting you'd get pleasure from helping bring them to justice." Wyatt sat his cup down and leaned forward.

Tony snorted with closed lips. "I'd like it a great deal. What do you need?"

"Great. Sit as you are and look out the door. Your employees are about to be walked through the other side of the bullpen. A stern glare as they stroll through wouldn't hurt." Wyatt winked at the stoic man.

Rizzo adjusted his seat sideways to get a better look, as Sanders and Coldwater paraded a few men through the bullpen. Coy James and Ben Thurman were among the group, separated by a couple of under-cover officers dressed in sloppy, street clothes, facing Wyatt's office, where their infamous CEO sat glaring.

Wyatt's glassed walls provided a perfect view. The two men visibly flinched and glanced at each other.

Rizzo played along, with his eyes shooting daggers their way while speaking quietly to Wyatt. "Those two assholes need to rot in hell."

The group was herded along a hallway into a lineup room, and the door shut behind them.

"Yeah, one way or another, they're going to prison. I appreciate your cooperation." Wyatt got his wish. The two had clearly witnessed Rizzo in his cubicle.

Wyatt stood, and Rizzo followed. Here's a shot of your daughter and me when we won state football championship in our senior year. Ava was a cheerleader, and I was quarterback. My mom took this shot." Wyatt retrieved the framed photo and handed it to Ava's dad. It displayed his younger, uniformed self lifting seventeen-year-old Ada into the air. She wore a cheerleader costume and a joyous smile.

"It's a lovely photograph and would make a fine addition to my family album." With emotion clearly in his eyes, Tony stroked his daughter's vision with a stubby, manicured finger.

"I'll make you a copy." Wyatt slid the photograph back into its spot.

"Thanks, Wyatt. From the angle, I must've sat near your mom at the game. I remember her. She's a lovely lady—your mother. I never missed a game my girl cheered at. You boys played well from what I recall, especially you and Levi Madison."

"Thanks. We did our best and had a blast." Wyatt leaned into his chair. "I'd like it if you hang out another ten minutes or so. Then you can take off. You've been a great help, and we appreciate your giving free reign of your books without a search warrant. It made our jobs easier."

Timing was everything, and the right moment could turn the tide. Rizzo angled it to see his men when they came out of the lineup. "It's not a problem, Wyatt. I'm on the side of the law and glad I did. I never suspected illegal activity going on inside my house. I'm happy to do whatever necessary to see the culprits serve time. Now I know those assholes altered the books and stole from me, I've hired a team of forensic accountants to get things cleaned up. I should thank you."

The lineup room door opened. Officers directed each of the men to different locations. Ben and Coy glanced into Wyatt's office once again before entering respective quarters.

Rizzo met their eyes. Glaring, he aimed a finger gun their way. Then he blew imaginary smoke from the barrel and winked.

Wyatt held back satisfied laughter itching to burst free. The terrified suspects looked like they'd wilt to the bullpen floor, and one of them might've soiled his pants.

"Well, Mr. Rizzo, that's all we need for now. I'll keep in touch. Don't become a stranger." Wyatt shook Tony's hand.

"Any time, Wyatt, it's a pleasure."

Once Tony was gone Wyatt entered the observation room to watch his deputy nail scumbags.

Leo and Jaiden entered Coy James' cubical. Sweat drizzled down his forehead. He swiped at it with a cuffed hand. "What the hell was that about?" Coy spat after waiting long enough to realize Leo wasn't going to start the conversation.

Cocking his head without changing his bland expression, Leo laughed. "What? The line up? I told you. We've got you and your buddy dead center for embezzlement. It's a given. You're going to rot in a cell for a long time for the crime. We're trying to nail down which of you dumb asses murdered Harvey Carnes. Our eye-witness was here to point out who did the deed. They've had a gander at you, and are speaking with another officer now. If you're the one, you best fess up if you want leniency. Otherwise, we're going after the death penalty, and neither of you gets a deal."

Coy's hands trembled rattling metal locking them together against stainless steel—a beautiful sound.

Leo leaned in his chair, rested his head in clasped hands, and crossed his ankles. Jaiden quietly watched and glanced away. She selected an emery board from a pocket and filed a jagged edge from her nail. Before putting the tool away, she aimed it at Ben like a weapon and did a mock trigger pull. Then she smiled satisfactorily and slid it into her back pocket.

Coy shivered and eyed her as though she was an alien creature. His gaze moved to Leo who ignored him. "Look, you guys. I was involved with the theft. Yeah. Ben came to me with an idea, but he's not the smartest dog in the pen. I helped flush out details of how it worked, and we did the theft together. Shit head Carnes poked his nose in everybody else's business and watched Ben like a hawk until he figured out our scam. We paid hush money to shut him up. That's all I was involved in."

"You're telling me, you have nothing to do with his murder? Sorry, I'm not buying it. Far as we're concerned you're both involved. We've got room for two of you on the death roster."

"Hell no. The little snitch was about to get us caught. Carnes was careless, wining and dining some slut; and was stupid enough to get caught in the sack by his wife. He threw around cash like tomorrow would never come. The wife was out to strip him of everything including his balls, so her attorneys dug into every aspect of his life. Of course they found the dough. Even if it didn't lead to us, the ass hole would've given us up sooner or later." Sweat dripped from his forehead, as he tried explaining his ploy.

"I get it, Coy. You had no choice. You and Ben concocted a plan and did away with old Harvey before he incriminated you. You certainly had good reason." Leo rolled an ink pen in his fingers. The dude thought it sounded reasonable.

Coy diverted his eyes drawing a big whiff of air. "I hear you. We had motive. But I didn't do it. We talked about how Carnes' screwing up posed danger for us, and Ben got nervous and scared. We heard about the blowout between Carnes' women, so Ben keyed one's car and knocked out lights in the other. He figured he was setting up a good opportunity to entice them get rid of the scumbag. I assumed one of his bitches killed l Harvey. If not, Ben must've gone off on his own and shot Carnes. I had nothing to do with the shooting."

Leo chewed the side of his mouth watching Coy twitch for a few minutes and enjoying a slight quiver in Coy's voice. "Nah, I'm not convinced. It sounds like the two of you plotted the deed. Then one of you—maybe Ben— pulled the trigger. Even if you didn't go to the house, you helped concoct the plan. I'll check with our person, to learn who they witnessed entering the Carnes residence the night he was slain." Before Coy uttered a word, Leo jumped and sped from the room with Jaiden on his heels.

Leo's belly did a happy dance, watching Coy through the mirrored wall. Sitting at his table, shoulders slung low, wringing his hands, his mouth opened wide.

"Got 'cha where I want 'cha." He spoke to the glass.

The two officers entered the second interrogation chamber where Ben slumped in his seat with his cuffed hands resting on the table. He attempted to right himself, but flopped forward. His cuffed hands were not chained to the table, only to each other.

"Ben, our witness saw you at Harvey Carnes' house the night he was murdered." Leo sat across from Ben, who looked ready to burst into tears, batting his eyes and not meeting the officers' gaze.

Jaiden took the second seat. "Yep, you'll get the death sentence, boy. Theft is small potatoes compared to murder one. Question is, are you the brains of the operation? Or did you have someone smart working with you? I'm not sure you've got guts to pull it off without support."

Finally after several minutes of silence, Ben glanced at Jaiden then eyed Leo, and his expression looked indignant, eyes narrowing and mouth pursed.

"I didn't need no body telling me what to do. I did Carnes myself. The little shit didn't deserve a penny. He was welcome to it if he'd acted discreet. But no. He had to play fast and fancy with the gals, throwing money around and talking too much to them women. He was fixing to get us arrested."

"So your partner, Coy James, came up with a plan to kill Harvey Carnes; and you pulled the trigger?" Leo locked his fingers together, knowing he'd already irritated the blundering fool.

"No, man. I don't need Coy James or no one else telling me what to do. I heard about Carnes' split-tails duking-it-out, and figured they'd like him dead. They might even do him for me. I set it up so they'd stay furious with each other and him for getting them in the situation. Them damned broads acted guilty, but they were all blow and no action. When I realized they weren't going to do it, I had to take care of Harvey myself. I never saw no witness the night I let myself in and shot the bastard. I didn't see no one."

Leo smiled congenially standing. "That's what I needed to hear. Thanks, Ben. We've got your admission on tape. Someone will type it up and bring it to you to sign."

Ben's chin quivered, and his brows pursed. "Them women had alibis. Huh?"

"No, matter of fact their alibis are shaky. We hadn't ruled them out—until now. Your confession clears them. Thank you for the confession."

Ben's shoulders shot back, like on some level he was proud of what he'd done. He shrugged. "Might as well, your witness picked me out from the lineup. I knew it was over when you put us in that room." He glanced away rocking his head back and forth.

"No. Actually, we didn't have a witness."

"But you said—" Ben's mouth flew open.

"Yeah, about that—I lied. How's that for a pile of crap?" Leo strode from the room.

Jaiden stood to follow him. With cuffed hands Ben gripped her arm. "Please, wait, you've got to help me. You promised mercy if I confessed."

Jaiden whirled around grabbed a finger and twisted it. The man cringed and leaned sideways. He tried spinning his body to keep up with his whirling appendage. Gasping, he held his breath spiraling as far as his cuffs allowed. When Jaiden stopped twisting his finger, he was lying with his shoulder against the side and his face toward the ceiling. A tear oozed from his moist eyes. She laughed and let go. He crumbled, face and hands against cold steel of the table.

"Did we, now? Was it another lie? Damn the bad luck. Look, asshole. You're going to prison, probably for life—if you're lucky. If not, they have a needle with your name on it. The state's attorney will take your admission into consideration, but we have no influence on the court system or with your jury. Where you're going, you'll want to be careful. Bad people thrive in those institutions. You pissed off a known mobster. Who knows how far Tony Rizzo's reach goes?" She looked him up and down. "They're going to like you in prison. Puny guys are popular, from what I hear." She slammed the door as she exited.

CHAPTER 21

"Hello." The deep, confident voice she recalled answered.

"Hi, Dad. Chloe, checking in. How's it going?" At her desk in the deserted real estate office, she practically held her breath. Her belly soured.

"Oh, Chloe, it's a surprise. I didn't expect your call. We're fine. You okay?" As always he sounded distracted.

Blyth's voice in the background badgered the twins to eat. "Are you helping me with these boys? Or not?"

"Yeah, hon, I'll get there in a sec. It's Chloe," he yelled happily with his voice away from the phone. "Chloe, Blyth sends her love and says *hi*."

Yeah. Sure. I heard—nothing.

"Sure, Dad, give her the same from me." *Bitch.* "You doing okay, Dad? We haven't talked for ages." Her heart ached for some acknowledgment he cared.

"I'm fine, busy. You doing all right? I understand you moved back to Sweetwater. How'd it go?" He sounded sidetracked. Curmudgeons in the background loudly chattered.

"I'm good. I'm buying a house. My offer was accepted today. Business is going well." Should she tell him about

225

the episode in Lexington? Her body trembled thinking of that jerk trying to physically force her to leave with him, an she didn't sleep the night before because of the cold feel of that gun barrel in her back.

"That's great, darling. Listen, can I call you back sometime? Blyth is having a bitch of a time getting the twins to eat. She needs help."

Those two chunky toddlers could stand to miss a meal.

"Sure, Dad, go on. Kiss 'em for me." She clicked off.

The wind had been knocked out of her. Dad would never return her call. It wouldn't occur to the blind fool Chloe had called because she needed him.

Grandpa Rizzo probably knew her better than her father. Reminiscing with Gran, meeting Tony and almost being abducted had left Chloe nostalgic, but calling Dad was a mistake making her feel worse.

The doorbell clanged, and Leo strode into the office. A bright smile framed his pearly whites, as he stepped lightly taking the few strides to her desk. Propping his tight, little butt on a corner, he reached for her hands.

"You look down?" His expression filled with concern. "It's no wonder, after that scene in Lexington."

"It's that and everything. I called Dad." It surprised her how her heart fluttered at his voice. His warm hands held hers securely, causing every nerve in her body to spark to life. What sensations would they cause cruising across her bare flesh, and why was she thinking of sex after all she'd experienced.

"Why does calling your Dad make you sad?" He brushed a tendril from her forehead.

She shrugged. "He's totally into his new family. There's no space in his life for me."

"That proves my instincts correct. Your dad was always a self-centered jerk. It's his loss. You're an amazing woman, Chloe. Someday he'll be sorry he didn't take time for you." His thumbs gently stroked, instinctively giving comfort.

"That's what Mom says. Somehow it sounds more convincing coming from you. Thanks, Leo." Leo had a soothing effect on her. She felt better already. His adorable boyish guise melted her icy mood. "What're you doing here, officer?"

"The Carnes murderer is in custody with a full confession. We solved an embezzlement case and there are kidnapping charges."

"What about Tray's dealings?"

"What can I say? Other than his connection to your grandpa—which you know is suspect in itself—Ackerson's dealings appear on the up-and-up far as we can tell. He just happens to be a pompous ass."

"I can't argue that." She nodded with a closed mouth smile.

"Our town is finally safe again, and I'm done working overtime. I'm hoping to convince you to celebrate with me." One hand brushed her cheek, circled her ear and glided below the cheekbone to her chin. "Please join me, Chloe." Her body tingled from the twinkle in his shiny, emerald eyes.

"How could I refuse?" He did want to be with her, after all. "As a matter of fact, I've got something to celebrate, too." After the debacle yesterday she deserved the contagious excitement filtering the air and a genuine smile took over her face. It felt good be a survivor, and her life was finally swinging in the right direction.

"I heard you and Ava reconnected with her father. It must be an amazing story. I hope to hear it one day."

So he wasn't going to press her for an explanation, unlike the lawman in Leo. She'd share her family secrets with him if things turned out well between them.

"I'm happy for you—all three of you." There was a definite *but* in there, obviously nervous about her grandfather's reputation.

"It's sweet, and it touches me deeply. Thanks for saying it. I understand your reservations. Believe me. I have my own. It's not what I'm celebrating. My offer on the house was accepted. I'll close in a couple weeks, sooner if the court complies." Joy flowed into her voice. Happiness was a choice she had made. She'd learned a trick or two in therapy to move forward and go on living. She shoved Dad's hurtful ways into a compartment where it belonged.

"Awesome; we're going somewhere special. Wear your finest duds. I'll pick you up in two hours." He dragged her to her feet, slipping his hands around her waist and tugged her against him. Her nipples hardened on contact.

Lean and hard against her, his utility belt around his slim waist added a certain thrill to the maneuver. A finger grazed across her lips. Her face eased into a happy smile, eager for what would follow. Soft, delectable lips massaged across hers gently at first, then with more vigor.

She met him with eager hunger. He tasted of mint and chocolate along with Leo's delightful signature flavor. Her breast pressed his firm belly, and her arms found their home around his neck holding him to her. They stayed like that for a good while, reveling in coming together after the agonizing wait. Snuggling in Leo's arms was worth every second of anticipation.

With a deep sigh and exhale he lifted his face, still holding her tight and rocked them side-to-side. His smile lit the room.

"I knew it would be this good. So good, I hate ending our delightful kiss-fest; but I want the evening to go perfectly so it's special and memorable. We'll celebrate your accomplishment and mine together. I can only bear to break away from you now because we'll do this again tonight and many, many times to come." His finger traced a line along her nose then her lips.

She nipped his fingertip. She could gaze into those gorgeous, glowing eyes joyously for the rest of her days. "I can live with that."

He edged away. "I'll pick you up in a little while."

"I can hardly wait. See you soon." Her eyes locked on his swaggering walk, as she watched him stroll away. Her mind filled with visions of snuggling against Leo with no fabric separating them.

♥♥♥♥

Almost ready for her date, Chloe donned her favorite ear rings as her phone chirped. Glancing at the screen, she steeled herself. "Hello, Tray. How are you?"

"I'm good, Chloe. I heard what happened at the Foundation Corporation yesterday. I'm glad you're alright. You are. Aren't you?"

"Sure, I'm fine. It could've turned out worse. Tony's and Leo's quick thinking helped me out of a jam. I was a basket case." She shivered at the recollection. Tray was probably happy to be let off the hook. With the case closed, Leo would no longer hound him.

"Really? Tony said you kept your cool in the hostage situation. It takes a hell of a woman to do that." Admiration accompanied his words.

Sentiments toward the debonair bachelor had soured, so his sweet-talk no longer worked on her. "Thanks, Tray. I didn't have a choice. I either did something rash or let the asshole drag me out of there. That was not happening." A chill sped down her spine reliving her terror.

"Let me take you to dinner." Funny, how he told instead of asked. It was his way, and no longer amused her.

"Thanks for the invitation. I'm going to pass. I'm seeing someone and want to give the relationship a chance. Can you and I remain friends and business associates?" She hated losing him as a client; but if he wanted, she'd willingly let him out of their contract.

"Deputy Sanders?" His voice sounded strained.

"Not your business, but yes. I'm seeing Leo."

He cleared his throat and spoke in a passive tone. "I figured as much. No worries between you and me. We're good. Live your life, Chloe. I wish you the best and hope it works out with Sanders. Let me know if the situation changes. I'm here for you." He coughed. "You will continue selling my properties, won't you?

"Absolutely and thank you; I appreciate it." There might be hope for the man yet, though he wasn't the man for her.

"Well, I'll let you go." He clicked off as the doorbell chimed.

CHAPTER 22

Leo resembled an adorable boy dressed in a tux for Sunday church. "Wow, Chloe, you knock my socks off. You're the prettiest, little filly I've laid eyes on." There's that drawl that thrilled her.

"Thank you, kind sir." She curtsied and spun. The full-skirt of her kelly-green, silk dress flowed out from her body. She'd chosen it because the dark color complimented her early spring tan and emphasized highlights in her hair, clipped in back so a cascade of curls fell behind one ear. She'd done everything in her power to look stunning for her date. His expression proved she'd achieved her goal.

He took her hand, and her world settled into proper alignment as they strolled to his truck. He lifted folds of fabric carefully onto the seat helping her into the tall cab. Then he climbed into the driver's side.

"Where are we going?" She felt giddy with eagerness, yet Leo's calm demeanor made her feel secure. He filled her world with serenity and touched her like she was a precious gem. She could face anything with him beside her.

"You'll see." He winked then snatched her hand and rested it on his thigh, covering it with his. The intimate act wasn't overtly sexual and simply felt right, like her palm had finally found its home.

His heart throbbed hard against her palm and enticing heat emitted from his grip. She resisted the urge to curl her fingers around his thigh moving closer to his crotch.

Sun set over the horizon minutes later, as he parked in front of what would soon become her new home. Her head rocked sideways, and she asked with her eyes.

Leo grinned. "No worries. I got permission from Mrs. Carnes."

She snickered, imagining Leo sweet talking the argumentative female. Without explanation, he helped her down, an they strolled through a side gate into the back yard. A small shelter had been erected holding a table and two chairs. Linens, flowers and candles decorated the setting of china and crystal for two.

Her heart caught in her throat, blocking her air, and she pushed back tears trying to fill her eyes. She hadn't realized Leo was a romantic.

Stepping to the back porch, Leo flipped a switch on an iPod and speaker system sitting there, and soft music played. The shelter, porch, fencing and surrounding trees held tiny, twinkling lights. A full moon ruled the night sky, as though ordered special.

"Oh, Leo, you surprise me. It's the most romantic thing anyone ever did for me. You're a passionate man with a tender heart." She gushed, spinning round and round. "It's like hundreds of stars orbiting in moonlight." Heady aroma filled the air. "Something smells amazing."

He stepped to a cart holding steaming, silver-covered containers. "I ordered from Dovie Fuller's restaurant. The food is fabulous. I hope you like French cuisine."

"I adore it. Dovie is a fantastic chef." He held a chair out. She slipped into it, and Leo took the other.

"We could've gone to the restaurant, but I wanted time alone to talk and get to know you better. I adore you,

Chloe. I tried to make this night extra special." His broad hands slipped over one of hers.

Warmth surged through her and found its home in her core, making her twist in her seat. Her soul opened to the man she'd spent a lifetime searching for.

There wasn't a doubt in her mind; they were meant for each other. Tonight was their perfect beginning.

He poured goblets of red wine and placed a tray of escargot on the table. "Your happiness is important to me. Everyone needs a bit of whimsy now and again, and you deserve the best. Something special is going on between us, Chloe. Tell me you feel it, too."

"I do, Leo; and this evening couldn't be better. Could it?" She wagged her brows comically, and they laughed. She was comfortable joking about it, recognizing longing in his eyes matching her desire.

Soft love songs crooned on the stereo. After sampling hors d oeuvres, he tugged Chloe to her feet. She melded against his frame and sighed. Cherished and contented in his arms, a thrilling craving seeped through her. It had been too long since she'd yearned for a man's attention.

He caressed her back holding her close. Heated fired passion melting her insides and tingling flesh of her neck. Her nipples hardened delightfully begging for attention, and a twitch shot between her thighs.

At the song's end they returned to their chairs. "You're quite the dancer for a country boy."

"Mom said if I wanted to impress a lady I had to make her feel special on the dance floor."

"She's a smart woman, and you've certainly done that." Would Leo introduce her to his family soon? Things seemed to be moving that direction, but she didn't want to push. They'd scaled enough hurdles for now.

They ate and caught up on events too long hanging between them. Conversation stayed light, and they steered away from topics that might screw up progress. Instead of being awkward, getting to know a new guy, it was a pleasure chatting with Leo.

"I talked to Tray."

"Yeah? How did it go?" He eyed her with an angled brow.

"Not bad. I explained I want to keep our relationship friendly and professional. He was a gentleman about it."

"I'm glad. He must be disappointed." When she did nothing more than smile, he winked. "I want you all to myself." Twinkle in his eyes filled her heart with joy.

She smiled and nodded. "Let's see where this thing between us leads."

"You didn't lose your listings. Did you?" Worry strained his gaze.

"No, Tray wants me to continue working for him."

"At least he's got some sense. I'm not going to pry, but are you in danger because of your grandfather?"

"I'll explain it sometime soon, but rest I'm not. He wouldn't be with us if there was any chance we'd be harmed."

"Good enough." He clasped her hands across the table. "You understand my concern. Right?"

"I do, but don't worry. I'm glad to have Tony around. He's certainly a character. Gran adores him and says he could charm panties off the Statue of Liberty. She rattles on and on about their sex life, which is apparently active and well due to the little blue pill. It's embarrassing, but she doesn't seem to notice. It's a symptom of her disease, so we let her go until we can't bear it any longer." Tears filled her eyes from the comedic aspect as well as grief over Gran's illness.

"I'm sorry about your Gran. It's a heart-breaking illness. Too bad there's no cure. She has a strong support system between you, Ava and Rizzo. By the way, Mr. Rizzo had an iron clad alibi. He was in New York the day Harvey died. He was a great help in solving the crime, but learning he was your grandfather was a shock."

"If you think you're shocked, let me tell you—you don't know the meaning of the word." Hopefully Leo could live with Tony's history. She wanted them both in her life. Her face screwed up. "Tony owns part of the company where my fiancé was employed. It concerned me, until I asked about it. He was unaware Hal worked there, until the police told him about the disappearance. He swears he knows nothing about it, and went so far as to hire an investigator when he heard Hal had vanished."

Leo looked like he was mulling the information over. Meeting her eyes, he smiled and shrugged. "Let's leave it at that. Is it okay with you?"

She exhaled. "Suits me." She believed Tony, and was glad Leo didn't make a fuss about him. She was determined to give them every chance to make it work with Leo, and the circumstances with Grandpa Rizzo was one less battle she didn't want to fight.

Leo held her hand, as they finished a bottle of wine then danced again. Leo bent his tall stature to her forehead and placed a tender peck on each eyelid. Then he nuzzled her nose. Her lips quivered with eagerness by the time he found them.

Their soft, gentle caress grew sent her libido soaring into overdrive, and she melted with longing for the tall, dreamy man. Having finally admitted to herself she'd fallen in love with him, she was holding nothing back.

His tongue delved inside her moist cavity, and she moaned as she imbibed blissfully in its divine silkiness. A responding surge of power to his already rigid rod throbbed against her belly. She leaned toward his erection, and his muscles quickened. A tightening in her groin evidenced her longing. The heavenly spell she'd slipped into was marvelous, and she never wanted it to end.

"Leo, I want you inside me. Make love to me." Her whisper breathed against his mouth.

He leaned enough to gaze into her eyes. "You're sure?"

She'd never wanted a man so desperately. Flame of desire burning wild built her nerve, and she nodded. "I never wanted anything so much. I need you."

He released her and flicked off the lights and music. Lifting her into his arms, he carried her to his pickup truck. Her head rested contentedly against a shoulder, and he gripped him around the neck, softly fingering his short haircut.

"What about all the stuff in the yard?" She was curious, but didn't actually care. She opened the door, and he sat her gently on the seat.

"Dovie's team will handle it." He closed the door. Then he joined her inside and placed her hand on his thigh. This time she gently massaged the sinuous muscle through his slacks.

"Where are we headed?" Her voice sounded unusually wistful.

"My place. Mom's keeping Cy for the night." His voice was low and gravelly, full of sentiment.

"Am I going to meet your mystery man, Cy?" She snuggled against him laying her head on his arm.

"I hope so. Spend the night with me." He glanced at her long enough to meet her eyes, and her breathe caught at the emotion in his. They'd crossed into the lover phase.

"I'd like nothing more than to wake in your arms." Intoxication of longing was a powerful spell she didn't want a cure for.

"I'll drive you home to change tomorrow. We can pick Cy up afterward, and you can meet Mom. We can spend the day together, if you're available. Cy's going to love you as much as I do." He brought her fingers to his lips and kissed the tips.

Leo loved her. She had fallen into another world, and never wanted to wake. She snuggled against her lover's shoulder, where she belonged.

"Perfect."

THE END

Dear Reader,

Thank you for reading my book. I hope you enjoyed it. If you did, it would please me a great deal if you'd drop me a short line at these review sites. I value your time, so feel free to copy paste the same review on both sites, if you would please. Reviews affect readership and are more important to me as an author than you can imagine. Thank you for your time, and I hope we become lifelong friends. Links are below.

https://www.bookbub.com/profile/lynda-rees   Bookbub
https://www.goodreads.com/author/show/17187400.Lynda _Rees   Goodreads

If you liked the book, you're going to love *The Bourbon Trail*, soon to be published. Here's a bit about it.

When her wealthy distiller lover is murdered, Ava Roberts and her dad, Tony Rizzo, become suspect, hindering her daughter, Chloe Roberts' love affair with Leo Sanders. Deputy Sanders is running the investigation, as the killer hungers for new blood.

Get it at: http://www.lyndareesauthor.com

ALSO BY LYNDA REES

Historical Romance:
Gold Lust Conspiracy
The Bloodline Series:
Leah's Story
Parsley, Sage, Rose, Mary & Wine
Blood & Studs
Hot Blooded
Blood of Champions
Bloodlines & Lies
Horseshoes & Roses
The Bloodline Trail
Real Money
The Bourbon Trail
Single Titles:
God Father's Day
Madam Mom
Children's Middle Grade:
Freckle Face & Blondie
The Thinking Tree
Find information about these books at website:

http://www.lyndareesauthor.com

Real Money
Bloodline Series Book 9

About Lynda Rees

Lynda is a storyteller, an award-winning novelist, and a free-spirited dreamer with workaholic tendencies and a passion for writing. Her dreams come true, blessing her with a supportive family. Whatever crazy adventure Lynda congers up, her loving Mike is by her side. A diverse background, visits to exotic locations, and curiosity about how history effects today's world fuels her writing. Born in the splendor of the Appalachian Mountains as a coal miner's daughter and part-Cherokee, she grew up in northern Kentucky when Newport prospered as a mecca for gambling and prostitution.

Published in romantic suspense, historical romance, children's middle-grade, advertising copy, and freelance, Lynda is an active member of several professional writing organizations and judge of professional writing events.

Author's Note:

Enjoy my work. I hope we become life-long friends. ***Time for Romance!***

Lynda Rees

Love is a dangerous mystery! Enjoy the ride.

Get the latest book deals, exclusive content and FREE reads by joining my VIPs. Email me for a FREE copy of *Leah's Story*.

Visit my website:

http://www.lyndareesauthor.com

Email: lyndareesauthor@gmail.com

Real Money
Bloodline Series Book 9

Made in the U. S. A., DeMossville, KY
Copyright © 2019, Sweetwater Publishing Company
DeMossville, KY 41033

CPSIA information can be obtained
at www.ICGtesting.com
Printed in the USA
LVHW021008121120
671417LV00012B/1249